Mrs. Alexander

Blind Fate

Vol. 3

Mrs. Alexander

Blind Fate
Vol. 3

ISBN/EAN: 9783337249618

Printed in Europe, USA, Canada, Australia, Japan

Cover: Foto ©Andreas Hilbeck / pixelio.de

More available books at **www.hansebooks.com**

A Novel.

BY

MRS. ALEXANDER.

AUTHOR OF

"THE WOOING O'T,"
"A LIFE INTEREST," "MONA'S CHOICE,"
"BY WOMAN'S WIT," "A FALSE SCENT," &c., &c.

IN THREE VOLUMES.

VOL. III.

LONDON:

F. V. WHITE & CO.,
31, SOUTHAMPTON STREET, STRAND.
1890.

CONTENTS.

BLIND FATE.

BLIND FATE.

CHAPTER I.

A TANGLED SKEIN.

THIS was a very trying time to Standish. He had an uneasy sense of being surrounded and played upon by forces he did not understand and could not control.

Unless Callander was absolutely insane, there must be some colour of reason under his sudden and extraordinary enmity against himself, and, seek as he might in all the holes and corners of his memory, Standish could not find the faintest shadow of a cause, even for fancied offence. Then, although not a little ashamed of giving heed to the whims of a young creature like

Dorothy, he could not quite steel his mind against the effect of her profound dislike and distrust of Egerton. What could have caused it? It was provoking of her not to confess all her reasons, if she had any, to him.

Finally, that somewhat tricky fellow, Dillon, was playing " fast and loose " with him in an audacious manner.

At any rate, he would bring him to book at once.

It was well, perhaps, that Standish was greatly occupied at the time, as, in addition to his work as précis writer to Lord R——, he had been promoted, which threw more upon his hands than he had had to do before.

This did not allow too much time for brooding over unsatisfactory puzzles, which seemed to grow more involved the longer he looked at them.

A line to Dillon brought that wily personage to Paul's lodgings in St. James's Place one evening, soon after the conversation last recorded.

Standish had returned from dining at his club in as bad a temper as his strong self-control would allow to take possession of him. He had an irritating notion that Dillon was the worst man he could have employed, that he had not taken any interest in the case, and had let any thread which might have led to detection slip through his fingers.

He had hardly taken off his coat and begun to look at an evening paper when Dillon was ushered in.

" Well," began Standish, rather impatiently, " I suppose that, as usual, you have no news for me ? "

" No sir — not yet," returned Dillon, giving him a quick, searching glance.

34*

"Come now—do you think there is any use in going on with the game? It has cost a good deal, and I see no chance of any result."

"Don't you, sir?"

"No—do you?"

"Yes! If I didn't, do you think I'd go on taking your money, or Colonel Callander's money? That's not my usual course—no play, no pay, is my maxim."

"Then have you any traces?"

"Traces! Ay, the scent is breast-high. Even if Mr. Egerton had not gone to Spain, I——"

"Then you think he'll catch the fellow?" interrupted Standish eagerly.

"Well, he may find the man he is gone in search of, or he may not. I've the threads in *my* hand. When I get just the one link that's wanting, I'll lay the whole evidence before *you*, Mr. Standish;

but until I have it, not one word will I speak."

"You are a curious fellow," returned Standish, looking hard at him, and thinking what a shrewd but low type of face he had. "If you can do this, I'll believe you are the cunning dog you are reported to be."

"Ay, I'll have the big reward yet, sir, and it won't be too big."

"Tell me; have you tracked this scoundrel, Pedro, through his wanderings?"

"Yes; I have tracked the murderer, and I can put my finger on him; but there is no use in doing that till my evidence is complete."

"Then why did you let Egerton undertake this wild-goose chase to Spain?"

"Why shouldn't I?" with a sneering smile. "It's just a ploy for a rich, idle man like him. What *he'll* find out is neither here nor there. He'll not find Pedro, and he knows it."

"Knows it?" echoed Standish. "What do you mean?"

"That Mr. Egerton was glad to get away from the talk and the bother of this wretched business, just to be quit of it all, and so he has shown you a clean pair of heels."

"I think you wrong him. No one could have shown more feeling and deeper interest than he has."

"Oh, I'll go bail he is interested enough. Isn't he going to give a thousand himself when we catch the murderer? Maybe it's a trifle more he'll be adding."

"By Heaven!" cried Standish, struck by the man's malignant smile. "You seem to suspect Egerton, himself. What confounded rubbish you are talking!"

"Suspect? Suspect an elegant, high-bred, honourable gentleman, too proud a'most to speak to the mere commonalty? Oh, no; I'm not quite so foolish; but you see, sir, it's my duty to suspect every living man, woman or child in or about the place on the night of the murder; and I *have* looked after every one of them."

"Myself included?" added Standish, with a slight derisive smile.

"You were in London," replied the detective coolly. "Of course you might have bribed the Spanish fellow, but things don't look like it. You don't suppose I'd ever find out much if I didn't think all men, from the saintliest parson up to the most noble dukes and earls, from the ploughman to the archbishop, capable of murdering everyone belonging to them if they had a strong enough motive? The very man you'd never suspect is, nine times out of ten, the real criminal. Human nature is a queer thing!"

"What a ghastly doctrine!" said Standish, slowly pulling his moustache.

"It's that, sir. But these kind of searches and speculations are uncommon interesting. If I were to write down all I have seen and known, everyone would cry out, 'What lies he is telling!'"

"You ought to write your memoirs, Dillon. It would be a valuable volume. Bentley or Longman would give you a long price for it."

"They will have to give it to my executors, then, for whatever I have jotted down, it shan't see the light till I am under the sod."

"A prudent resolve, no doubt. Well, then, Dillon, I am still to leave matters in your hands, unquestioned, until you are pleased to reveal all you know?"

"Just so, sir. It won't be long; but 1 cannot fix a time. I may get at what I want to know to-morrow or next day; I may not hit it off for three weeks or a month; but, sooner or later, I'll have the whole story clear."

"Do you expect us to be greatly surprised?"

"Well, I would rather not say, sir."

"Have you seen Colonel Callander since his return?"

"Yes; just once."

"He is terribly broken."

"Ay, that he is," and something like a gleam of compassion shot across his hard face. "He will never be the same man again."

"I fear not! He is thinking of going to Fordsea, I find."

"Is he?" with sharp, suddenly roused attention. "That's a trip won't do him much good. Do you know when he goes down?"

"I am not sure; he may take the whim any day."

Dillon thought for a moment in silence, and Standish said, "You did not think the evidence of that sailor, Ritson, of any consequence?"

"Not much," replied Dillon, rousing himself from his meditations. "He only told us what we knew before. We certainly got at the size and look of the man who laid the ladder across, but if it was the Spanish chap, why, you all say he was like Mr. Egerton in size and build."

"True!" and Standish did not speak again for a few seconds; then he exclaimed, "I have detained you long enough, and I ought to dress and go out"

"All right, Mr. Standish; it's me that is

keeping you." He rose as he spoke from the chair where he had been sitting at what might be termed a civil distance from Standish. " By the by," he resumed, pausing, " How is the young lady ? "

" Which young lady ? "

" The little brown-haired lady with the eyes that tell you everything without her opening her lips," he ended, with a low peculiar laugh.

Standish frowned. " You mean Miss Wynn. Pray, is she among your suspected ? "

" Not now. She is an uncommon shrewd young lady, she is," continued the detective. " Ah ! she took it all desperate hard, and she doesn't like me a bit too well. She looks at me, half afraid, like a startled fawn. One might think she was frightened for what I might find out."

" That is an imaginative flight on your

part, Mr. Dillon. I must wish you good evening."

" Good evening, sir. I'll let you know the minnte I have anything clear and satisfactory to tell."

" Satisfactory," repeated Standish, when he was alone. " He has a curious idea of what is satisfactory. He is like a ghoul, revelling among the ghastly skeletons of his ungodly secrets ! I wonder what he is at ? It is absurd, but I am half inclined to share the fright he attributes to Dorothy. But what *can* he find out, except the miserable scoundrel who cut off Mabel's fair life for the sake of her few jewels."

Instead of dressing to go out, Standish donned a smoking jacket, and sat down to think.

His interview with Dillon had disturbed him out of all proportion to anything that

had transpired during it, and at last, growing feverish, he turned from the subject by
a strong effort of will, and applied himself
to write an abstract of some papers for his
chief. It was a serious deprivation to him
to be cut off from his almost daily visits
to Prince's Place. But so long as there
was any risk of encountering Callander, he
thought it right to abstain from going
there. It was astonishing what a blank
this created in his life. He had been quite
comfortable and contented for years, and
now a strange restlessness and dissatis-
faction had fastened upon him. He must
get rid of these morbid feelings. The
painful death of his young ward had un-
hinged him. He must not yield to this
sort of womanish weakness.

It was the day after this interview that
Mrs. Callander honoured her niece with a
visit. Henrietta was dressed to go out

when the Dowager's carriage drove up. With a little grimace expressive of resignation she took off her fur-lined cloak and laid it over a chair as Mrs. Callander was announced, and that lady entered attired in the richest and blackest mourning that could be invented.

"My dear Aunt! I am delighted to see you—so glad I had not gone out, do sit down by the fire."

"Not too near, thank you! I never have accustomed myself to indulgence! I intended to have called upon you sooner, Henrietta. I wished to see how you were placed. You are well aware I never approved of this scheme of yours of living by yourself with so insignificant a companion as Dorothy Wynn."

"Well, I don't see what else I could have done. Those poor children wanted a home —and——"

"You could have joined me with them," interrupted Mrs. Callander.

"And left poor Dorothy alone? No— that would never have done! You forget that Herbert wished her to be with them."

"Herbert's infatuation is something I cannot understand! He seems to think that mere girl more deserving considera- tion than his mother. Every one is thought of in preference to *me!*" and her voice rose to a shrill tone of distress.

"It is very curious," returned Henrietta, sympathetically, but not perceiving all her exclamation admitted.

"I suppose that is the reason my grand- children are never sent to see me," con- tinued the old lady querulously.

"Poor old thing! how grey and miser- able she looks!" thought her niece. "But they went to Somerset Square last week," she said aloud.

"Last week, Henrietta! Am I to be put off with a stated weekly visit? Do you think that my son's children are not always welcome to me, though their mother was the last person I should have wished him to marry?"

"Poor dear Mabel! Well, aunt, she will never offend you more."

"I know what you mean, Henrietta! that I was hard and unkind to her. But I was only just and honest. I am terribly shaken by her awful end, though I am sure if we could get at the truth, you would find it was greatly her own fault! Her careless, reckless way of leaving her jewels and valuables about for wandering vagabonds to see! In fact, she was not accustomed to such things, and did not know how to take care of them."

"How can you talk in that way, aunt? Hush! here is Dorothy."

Mrs. Callander drew herself up, as Dorothy came in. Her pale face, sad earnest eyes, and slight fragile figure might have touched Mrs. Callander's not very impressionable heart, but for the idea of the preference shown by her son for his sister-in-law, this made her adamantine to Dorothy and almost to her favourite niece.

"How do you do, Mrs. Callander?" said Dorothy, advancing to her, her eyes full of kindly feeling, for she deeply sympathised with the proud old woman in the mortification her son's avoidance must inflict.

"I am *not* quite well, I thank you. Indeed I doubt if I shall ever be myself again. Few mothers have been more sorely tried," and she pressed her black-bordered handkerchief to her eyes.

"I am *so* sorry," Dorothy was beginning, when Henrietta broke in. "My aunt is vexed because the children do not go often enough to see her."

" Oh, Mrs. Callander, they shall go as often as ever you like. I thought they might give you more trouble than pleasure or they should have gone every other day ! ''

" I see no reason for your concluding that I was indifferent to my son's children," testily. " Indeed the more proper and natural arrangement would be to have given the poor children into *my* care ! You must feel yourself that you are too young."

" Ah ! Mrs. Callander, I feel old enough for anything," exclaimed Dorothy, " and my dear lost sister would have chosen me before anyone else to take her place with her little ones, but I know that you have a claim too — only don't try to take them from me ! They are all I have left," and her big eyes filled with tears.

"Take her place," repeated Mrs. Callander to herself. "Thank God that horrid, blasphemous, revolting 'deceased wife's sister's bill,' will never pass, or Heaven only knows what would happen." She only said: "You are very good I am sure to admit I have any 'claim,' as you call it, whatever!"

Dorothy sighed. She could not answer this cruelly disappointed, unjust, exacting woman sharply—she felt too much for her.

"I am sorry the children are out, but they shall go to you to-morrow. Would you like them before or after luncheon?"

"Send them before luncheon and I will bring them back, or Miss Boothby will," returned the dowager, a little softened.

"Now, Henrietta, I must say you have a

35*

very indifferent house. The entrance is decidedly mean, and the stair is dark."

"Well, Aunt Callander, it costs quite enough, and you know I had to think of Herbert's pocket as well as my own, still I flatter myself the drawing-room is pretty."

"It is full of twopenny - halfpenny decorations I grant; now you *ought* to have reception rooms adorned with few but massive and valuable ornaments, not frippery, like this."

"Well, I don't like that style of funereal chamber. Dorothy and I have been miserable enough to value brightness even in such humble guise as a sixpenny fan or two."

Mrs. Callander elevated her chin contemptuously.

"I should like to see the children's apartments," she said haughtily.

"Oh, yes. Henrietta, will you take Mrs.

Callander to the nursery ? " said Dorothy,
hesitating whether she should go or stay,
and deciding that it would be more agreeable to the dowager if her niece only
accompanied her.

She drew near the fire, and leaning her
head against the mantel-piece, she thought
how terrible it would be if Herbert were
ever persuaded to give the children into
Mrs. Callander's care. What would become
of her ? for to live with them in the dowager's house would be impossible ! And she
could not trust poor Herbert in his present
condition. If he took such an amazing
unaccountable dislike to Paul Standish,
why, she herself might be the next object of
his aversion. How uncertain her own
future seemed ! If—if only she could
keep with the children, she might settle
into resignation and content. As to Mrs.
Callander, odiously disagreeable as she

made herself, she could not help compassionating her, for it must be a great trial to see a son, a beloved son, turn from you with scarcely veiled coldness—nay, more, with positive repulsion. Surely she was punished for any unkindness she had shown Mabel!

" They are decidedly poky, stuffy rooms," observed Mrs. Callander, returning, followed by Henrietta. " Now in *my* house they might have a whole floor—light, airy, dry, suitable in every way. It is useless, however, to say anything. My son—ah, there he is! " Seizing a photograph which stood on Henrietta's writing table, she sat down and gazed at it for a moment, then she exclaimed in trembling tones : " Ah ! it is too—too hard to think of the way he has treated me through all this time of his sorrow—as if I were unworthy to share it ! " and threw the photograph from her, with difficulty restraining her tears.

"You ought to consider how changed he is," said Dorothy, softly. "I am sure that his late illness and overwhelming grief have changed him a great deal. He is not like himself. See how he has turned against Mr. Standish, who used to be such a favourite with him, and is always——"

"I do not consider *that* a mark of insanity," interrupted Mrs. Callander; "I never thought Mr. Standish a good companion nor a good influence for Herbert. He is a cold, selfish, atheistical worldling, ready to scoff at everyone and everything superior to himself. I always deplored his intimacy and familiarity in Herbert's house, a man of whose principles I am more than doubtful, and——"

"Mrs. Callander," said Dorothy, gravely, "you must not speak against my guardian

before me! He is the best and only friend
I have, and I cannot listen to anything
against him. He has been a father to
Mabel and to me. A truer gentleman in
every sense does not exist. I never could
understand why you disliked him."

" Perhaps it is better, at your age, that
you should not," returned Mrs. Callander,
significantly.

Dorothy gazed at her, puzzled and
amazed.

" Indeed, Aunt, Paul Standish is a capital
fellow; I think you are very unjust to him,"
cried Henrietta.

" I repeat, that my opinion is fixed and
well-founded, but if neither of you like the
expression of it, I need not trespass any
longer on you. Your obstinacy and in-
credulity passes the ordinary folly of young
people."

" I should be sorry to fail in the respect

due to you, Mrs. Callander, said Dorothy, firmly, though her heart beat fast, "but I never will listen to a word against Mr. Standish."

"Your respect or disrespect is of small moment," returned the Dowager, rising. "Your insignificance is—is such that I do not care to answer you." She rose, and, turning to her niece, said shortly, "I wish to see the children about eleven to-morrow morning," and without further speech she left the room.

"What a cantankerous old soul she is to be sure," cried Miss Oakeley, looking out of the window to see the Dowager's equipage drive off.

"Yes; but how ill and broken she looks!" said Dorothy. "Why does she despise me so much?"

"Oh, it is only her cross-grained way of talking ; you should not mind her."

"I do not, indeed. My self-esteem is strong enough to withstand such attacks; but her dislike to Paul is quite inexplicable. What did she mean by saying I had better *not* understand?"

"Heaven knows! But, Dorothy, you are a loyal, plucky little soul. I was delighted with you for standing up to her highness so gallantly in defence of Mr. Standish!" and Henrietta put her arm round Dorothy's neck.

"Yes, of course. What else could I do?"

Henrietta did not answer immediately; she began to play with the ends of her black sash, and removed her arm from Dorothy's neck. They were standing on the hearthrug, Dorothy having her back to the light. Henrietta seemed in deep thought, and was looking down, with a slight, peculiar smile playing round her mouth. Something in her expression made Dorothy wonder what she was thinking of.

"Tell me," exclaimed Henrietta, so suddenly that Dorothy started; "have you observed any change in Mr. Standish of late?"

"A change? How do you mean?"

"I mean in his manner, his style, his looks generally."

"No, Henrietta; I do not think I have. Why?"

"Well, I suppose *you* would be the last to perceive it. I suppose he seems quite old to you; and always looking on him as a sort of father, it would never occur to you that he could fall in love!"

"No; certainly it never did occur to me, but, of course, there is no reason why he should not."

"Exactly. Now who do you think he has fallen in love with?"

" How can I tell? I never see him in society."

" Why, Dorothy, what a little goose you are! *I* have seen for some time that he is rather smitten with myself! Now do you see ? "

" Well, no, Henrietta, not exactly. To be sure, I have not had such pleasant thoughts in my mind as love and lovers ! "

"For some weeks," resumed Henrietta, " I have noticed a great change in his way of speaking and looking, and——Sit down by me here on the sofa, and I will tell you everything. I have the greatest confidence in your good sense, young as you are, Dorothy. It was about a week ago, after Mr. Standish had tried to get an explanation from Herbert, and he was standing there with his elbow on the mantel-piece, looking glum and solemn (you were out

shopping with Nurse), so I said, ' What
are you thinking of, Mr. Standish?' He
turned to me with *such* a look! He hasn't
what are called handsome eyes, but they *can*
speak, and said he: 'You must know very
well what I am thinking of, Miss Oakeley!
How utterly miserable this whim of Callander's makes me! I had grown so used
to come in here and feel at home, that I
seem lost without this delightful asylum,'
—or words to that effect. Then I began
to understand other words and looks of his
that had puzzled me a good deal. I only
said that we missed him dreadfully, and
that he ought not to mind Callander. At
this he went on to talk of the influence I
had over poor Herbert in a sort of half
jealous strain. Wasn't that remarkable?"

"I think it is natural enough," said
Dorothy, seeing she paused for a reply.

"You dear little soul! You think too

much of me," kissing her. " Well, be that as it may, I have noticed many little things since that quite convince me he is rapidly falling in love with me. It is a way men have. You would be surprised how many people have proposed to me, or, let me see, they would like to propose. Oh! I know ill-natured people say it is because I have a tolerable fortune, but, candidly speaking, I really do not think it is. I am no beauty, I know that quite well, but I can't help feeling that there is a certain charm about me. Now, as to Paul Standish, I am sure he is perfectly disinterested, and after hesitating over endless suitors, I don't think I could do better than take him. He is quite charming, and old Sir Mark Pounceford told me the other day that he is a very rising man. Now you can't do much or rise high without money, and my fortune will be of the greatest use to him.

I should enjoy being an ambassadress one of these days; so you see, it would be a very suitable marriage."

"Yes," said Dorothy, rather mechanically, and, remembering Paul's eulogium on her friend in their last confidential walk, she added, "I believe he does love you."

"Then even you see it!" cried Henrietta joyfully. "I thought I knew the symptoms too well to be deceived. You'll see, Dorothy, what a nice, kind, pleasant guardiana (that's a good word) I will be to you. I daresay it seems very strange to you that I should take a fancy to Paul Standish, he must seem quite elderly to you; but I really have. You see, he is very *distingué*, and he seems so nice and devoted that I feel quite fluttered when he comes into the room. Of course, I am much nearer his age than you are. I don't mind confessing to you that I am a little past thirty.

Imagine! I was more than ten years old
when you were born. Yes, indeed! Let
me see, who was my governess, then? Oh,
Mademoiselle Delaporte! She was rather
nice. Oh, I have had such a string of
governesses. I fancy I gave them all a
great deal of trouble. One thing we are
alike in, Dorothy. We never knew what
it was to have a mother. We were just
shunted about from one deputy parent to
another—at least, I was."

"Oh! how delightful it must be to
have a mother — even to remember a
mother!" said Dorothy, in a low, dreamy
tone, "I felt that whenever I saw dear,
sweet Mabel with the babies. The very
way she touched them and looked at them
was so different from Mrs. McHugh and
Peggy, kind and good as they are. Can I
ever fill her place to her children?"

"To be sure you can! You are the

tenderest-hearted girl I ever met, except, in-deed, to poor Mr. Egerton," cried Henrietta lightly. "Never mind, dear, Paul Standish and I will find you an ideal husband, rich, and handsome, and débonnaire, and all that Dorothy's spouse ought to be. Now, I have stayed talking much too late. I pro-mised the Blackburns to be with them about four. Good-bye for the present. Mind, all I have said is under the rose—oh! a dozen roses."

Dorothy remained sitting where Henrietta left her for some minutes, one arm out-stretched and resting on the end of the sofa, the hand drooping, the other hand pressed against her cheek. For some moments her thoughts were all in painful confusion. Gradually the full sense of all Henrietta had been saying dawned upon her. Yes, it was all quite true. They were well suited in age, position, circumstances.

Henrietta's fortune would be a great help
to Paul, and Paul was evidently fond of
her. She had been much struck by the
heartiness of his praise the last time they
had spoken of her, and Henrietta was good,
and generous, and kind. Oh, yes! but
how—how would Paul bear her endless,
thoughtless chatter about herself, her
doings, her dress, her careless, incon-
sequent flights from subject?—all this
would distract him. Yet Henrietta must
know what she was talking about. Oh!
how could she talk so when everything
was yet uncertain? If they married, how
earnestly Dorothy hoped they would be
happy. But for herself, what an awful
sense of desolation fell upon her. Hence-
forth, she would be quite alone, a mere
secondary object to everyone, even the
children might be taken from her, and
Paul, her dear, kind guardian, would no

longer have the same thought or tenderness to bestow upon her. He would be kind and true always, but the full feast of his confidence, his care, his unstinted sympathy, could be hers no longer. She must accept as thankfully as she could what crumbs might fall from Henrietta's amply furnished table. She rose noiselessly, and creeping away to her own room, wept long and bitterly, till shame at her own prostration lent her strength to compose herself.

36*

CHAPTER II.

SINCE Colonel Callander returned to London, Collins, his soldier servant, contrived, with more or less success, to serve two masters, or rather a master and a mistress.

He generally addressed Miss Oakeley at breakfast, two or three times a week, with " If you please, ma'am, I'm going over ' to do ' for the Colonel this morning," or " If you have any message, ma'am, I'll be at the hotel between eleven and twelve." He never pretended to ask leave. The Colonel's service was, in his mind, a supreme duty which swallowed up all others.

Collins would have laid down his life for his master. He thought him the truest of

men, the finest of gentlemen. Nor was
Collins alone in his opinion. The unhappy
man, who at this period of his history was
overweighted with a broken heart and
diminished brain power, had always been
best loved by those who knew him longest,
and no one, perhaps, save his faithful
attendant, perceived how profound was the
change which sorrow and suffering had
wrought in his revered master.

He fully shared the dread with which
Dorothy contemplated her brother-in-law's
intended visit to Fordsea, and, impelled by
a dim anticipation of possible danger, had
ventured to ask permission to accompany
him. This was immediately refused, so
Collins was fain to satisfy himself by packing his master's valise, and re-arranging his
belongings, as Miss Oakeley had persuaded
Callander to establish himself in an hotel
much nearer to her abode than Dover

Street. He resolutely rejected both her own and his mother's offers of hospitality.

Collins therefore betook himself earlier than usual on the morning of the day Callander was to leave town, and had been in time to take a few instructions from his master and hand him his hat and gloves.

"Ah! he'll never be like himself again," thought Collins, when he closed the door after him and began to empty the contents of a wardrobe and a large box on the bed and a table at its foot. "He treats me like a stranger, he sometimes doesn't seem to know who he is speaking to—Ay! those devils took more than a few rings and bracelets, they stole a brave fellow's heart and smashed it up the night they murdered my poor dear lady! I'd like to half hang 'em, cut 'em down, and hang 'em over again, I would!" He was proceeding to "sort" his master's things as he thought thus—and

had the Spanish sailor who had committed
the crime suddenly appeared, his shrift
would have been a short one.

"Come in!" shouted Collins almost
angrily, still under the influence of these
thoughts, as a tap on the door caught
his ear. It opened, and Dillon the detective
presented himself.

His appearance at that moment was most
welcome to Collins, who, laying down the
coat he was folding, greeted him warmly.

"The Colonel has just gone out, Mr.
Dillon. I wonder you didn't run up
against him."

"The porter was not quite sure whether
he had gone out or no, so I just stepped
up to see. I am sorry I missed him. I'll
call again in the evening."

"Then you'll not see him, Mr. Dillon, for
he's off by the six train for Fordsea!"

"For Fordsea!" echoed the detective, and

he seemed to think very seriously. " Are you going with him ? "

" No,—worse luck. I think he'd be the better of a careful man beside him! Will you sit down, Mr. Dillon ? May I make so bold as to ask if you have any news to tell ? "

" Well, not much," taking a chair, and eyeing the varied collection of clothes, books, impedimenta of all kinds, spread out before him, keenly, " and that, much or little, I can only tell by-and-by. It is perfectly amazing how mere whispers ooze out."

" That's true—you'll not mind me going on with my work. I want to finish up and pay up before one o'clock to get back for my young ladies' lunch."

" Oh, don't mind me, Mr. Collins. I'm sure it's pleasant to see how fine and orderly you settle them all. What a lot of fine things! Does your boss always carry an arsenal like that about with him? I suppose they are curiosities?"

"Not the pistols, they are in prime working order—some of these are things he has bought abroad, I daresay," pointing to one or two small scimitars, etc., which he was about to put in the bottom of a large trunk.

"You see," continued Collins, "the gentry must be doing something, and when they are travelling, between the journeys and going though the churches, and eating at the *table-d'hôte*, they have nothing to fill up the time with, but going into dusty, fusty shops, and buying everything they can lay their hands on."

"That's true! It's easy to see *you* have not gone about with your eyes shut. Didn't some of these come from India?"

"Ay, the pistols did, and that 'ere

crooked sword, the others he brought back from Germany just now. I never saw them before."

" The Germans mostly put a mark on them," said the detective, taking one up and carrying it to the window, where he examined it for a minute or two and then returned it carelessly to Collins. " Yes, it's German make, and very old," he said.

" I suppose you have seen most things," observed Collins admiringly. " Have you found out many murders, may I make so bold as to ask?"

" Ay, a goodish few ! I could write a curious book about them."

" That you could, I'll go bail! It would be fine reading."

" Yes, it might if the subject were treated philosophical! There's a deal of character in the way people set about a murder! I think I could tell pretty nearly from a

man's face and build, how he would set
about his murders !"

"Would you now ?" said Collins, pausing
in the act of wrapping up a pair of boot
trees, and listening with awe.

"Yes, there is yourself," looking sharply
at him.   "It would be a 'draw and defend
yourself' sort of business with *you*.   Then
you'd fight fierce enough, till one or the
other were done for."

"Well, Mr. Dillon, I wouldn't call that
murder !   Would you ?"

"Out west we'd call it—not murder—
certainly, but in England they would be
apt to hang you for it !   Then there's a
class of men who stick you in the back,
others make believe their victims kill themselves, that's what you might call the
intellectual class of murder, it takes just
a pile of planning and thinking out.   I
have had some very interesting cases of

that kind through my hands! Women go in largely for poisoning. Lord! how long and carefully and delicately they'll contrive —ay, for months and months—before they finish their business! You see nature has given some of 'em cunning and invention to make up for want of strength."

"Bless my heart! it makes me feel creepy to hear you talk! Well, the man that struck our poor lady must have been a cowardly villain. How he could hurt her in her sleep!"

"Probably she began to stir, and he thought she would wake and scream, and he would be caught! so he silenced her for ever. Burglars seldom take life if they can help it, but this fellow was a stranger probably, and did not know the ways of the place."

Here the door again opened—this time to admit Mrs. McHugh, who had a parcel

in her hands and a displeased expression
on her face.

"Oh! good morning, Mr. Dillon!" then
turning sharply on Collins she went on.
"Sure you were in an extra hurry this
morning to go off and never remember to
come up to me for the master's shirts,
there wasn't a button left on them by that
limb of a laundress. Now I have had
to come the whole way myself. For I
was not sure what time he would set out,
and as to trusting that girl!——" Only
a sudden pause could express the depths of
her deficiencies!

"Well, ma'am, it's an ill wind that blows
nobody good," said the detective gallantly.
"If you hadn't been obliged to come
around I should not have had the pleasure
of seeing you."

"You're very polite, I am sure!"
returned Mrs. McHugh with an audible

sniff, "and *I* am glad to have an opportunity of asking you if you have done
anything or if you ever intend to do anything? I am sure, from all Mr Standish
said of you to Miss Dorothy and me, I
thought you'd catch the cunningest thief
of a murderer that ever burrowed under
the earth, or dived under the sea! and
here, near six months have passed, and
you haven't laid your finger on him yet!
Considering we know, in a manner of
speaking, who the cruel scoundrel is—it
isn't such a tremendous task to find
him."

Mrs. McHugh from extreme awe of, and
faith in, Dillon's untried powers, had passed
to the opposite extreme of doubt, deepen-
ing into utter distrust and contempt.

"I'm sorry to see you have such a
poor opinion of me, ma'am," said Dillon,
with mock humility, which enraged his

interlocutor who was too shrewd not to perceive his real indifference to her opinion. "However, I'm not quite done with the business."

"No, I don't suppose you will be till Mr. Egerton finds the wretch in Spain."

"Well, ma'am, you'll admit that Mr. Egerton has a few advantages over me. Yet, somehow, I don't think he'll have any better success. Come, now, what'll you bet that I land the fish first?"

"Betting is not in my line, and I think too highly of a kind, good, generous gentleman like Mr. Egerton, to make a bet about him."

"Ay, just so! he is all that. *Re*-markably open handed, and highly moral, a man you'd trust your life to, hey?"

"Yes, I would," said Mrs. McHugh, looking at him sternly, "and I'm sure I don't know what you mean by talking in a sneering way of such a gentleman, a gentleman whose money you know the touch of, I'll go bail!"

To her mortification the detective burst out laughing.

"No, ma'am, not *yet!* but I daresay I may have the handling of some of it before the year is much older. Now, I am afraid I must tear myself away from pleasant company. Aint't I unlucky, Mr. Collins, to miss the Colonel? However, I can wait a bit to see him. Good morning Mrs. Mc-Hugh! I hope I'll recover my place in your opinion before I die. Good morning, Mr. Collins." With a nod and a curious triumphant chuckle, Dillon left the room.

"Well, he is unlucky," said Collins, opening the parcel Mrs. McHugh had brought. "He has been six or seven times if he has been once to see the Colonel, and he is never in."

"Then mark my words, Collins. He don't want to find him!"

"I think you are wrong, Mrs. McHugh, and you'll excuse my mentioning it, but I would not speak so sharp to him if I was you. He's a wonderful man, that Dillon. He knows what's inside your head a'most before you do yourself. He'll tell you the sort of murder you'd commit, by looking in your face. He——"

"He would turn *you* inside out, I daresay," said Mrs. McHugh, loftily, "but I'd like to hear him telling *me* the sort of murder I'd commit! Set him up! It's pretty plain the sort of company he is used to. I'm surprised at a clever man like Mr. Standish believing in him. He is just hanging on, spending the master's money, eating and drinking of the best, and pretending he's that deep that no one can fathom him. If anyone ever catches that

bloodthirsty villain, it will be Mr. Egerton,
and Dillon knows it ; that's why he is so
spiteful against him. To be waiting full
six months for justice on the wretch that
robbed those precious children of their
sweet mother ! Don't tell me a detective
that is so long settling a job is worth his
salt.   I'll never know a peaceful hour
till I see that monster hung. Yes, I'd go
see him swing ! "

"Well, I don't blame you, Mrs. Mc-
Hugh. Still, I think Dillon knows a good
bit. It's my belief he's playing a deep
game, and he'll surprise you some day, no
—no--he is wide awake. Look at his
eyes——"

" I'd rather not. They are like ferret's.
Well, there are the shirts, a dozen, and not
a button wanting to one of them. Ah,
Collins ! It makes me heart ache to look
at the poor dear master ! He is that lov-

ing to the children one minute, and can't bear the sight of them the next! It was too happy we were! To see the poor mistress and Miss Dorothy, just like loving angels, and the Colonel and Mr. Standish like brothers; sure, the cruel, envious evil spirits must have got the upper hand for an unlucky hour, to blight it all with their devilish spite. I must get back for the children's dinner. I suppose you won't be long?"

"Well, it will be a good half-hour, but I'll come as soon as I can."

  *   *   *   *   *

Standish naturally took advantage of Colonel Callander's absence, to renew his visits to Prince's Place. He was far too sensible to take offence at the whims of a man so evidently out of mental harmony, and he was anxious to see as much as he could of his interesting ward, whose mood puzzled and distressed him. In all her grief and depression, she had always spoken to him with the utmost confidence, with a degree of unreserve which showed how glad she was to open her heart to him. But for the last week she had grown silent, reserved, hesitating—she seemed to think before speaking to him.

This change worried him more than he confessed even to himself. It set him thinking of the time, before their great sorrow, when she had peremptorily refused Egerton, and revived the question which had then frequently presented itself: "Has Dorothy any girlish fancy for anyone, who perhaps does not return it, or has amused himself, and passed by?" He had in some occult way always felt Dorothy to be more companionable, more mature, than her elder sister.

He often found unexpected depths in her quickly developing mind, and felt sure that, though proud and maidenly enough, she was sufficiently individual to form a decided liking apart from that waiting "to be chosen" which is the conventional type of womanly feeling, but she was sufficiently strong also to hide it, though not to trample it down without suffering, and he loved his lonely little ward too well to contemplate such a possibility without keen distress.

Yet, he knew her simple life so well, that he wondered he could not fix upon the man who had attracted her. Could it have been that pleasant young sailor who was of their party to Rookstone? She saw so very little of him, she could hardly have much feeling about him. Should he ask her? Standish knew human nature well enough to be aware

that confidence is rarely given in reply
to a point-blank question. No, he must
try and win it. " If there are any difficulties between her and the man she may
possibly love, I will do what I can to
smooth them. I trust in God she hasn't
given her heart to a scamp! It is quite
possible. Love is an awfully dangerous
game for so young a creature. Why,
Dorothy will not be twenty till the end of
July, and it seems but yesterday that she
came with pride to show me her first long
frock. If I had made a boyish marriage,
which, thank God, I did not, she might
have been my daughter."

So pondering, Standish reached Prince's
Place, and was shown upstairs to the
drawing-room, where he found Miss
Oakeley.

Still further upstairs Dorothy was amusing her little nephew and niece, as the chill

February afternoon was too showery and east-windy to allow of their going out. Mrs. McHugh sat at her needlework, while "auntie" built up card houses for "Boy" to knock down.

"Isn't he silly?" cried Dolly, as the riotous little fellow held his chubby hands ready to level the structure before the second story was quite finished. "Be quiet, you naughty boy; let us see if auntie can make it much—much higher."

"Naughty! Dolly naughty!" he exclaimed, rising on the foot-board of his chair to slap his sister with right good will.

"For shame, Master Herbert! to strike your sister. That's not like a gentleman."

"Let me build one quite high house, darling, and you shall knock down the rest," and the process went on for a few minutes.

"And is there no news at all of Mr. Egerton?" asked Nurse, breaking a tolerably long silence, while she threaded her needle.

"Mr. Standish had one letter from him, soon after he had reached Valencia, before he had time to do anything, but he has not written since, though he promised to do so!"

"Well, to my mind, he is the likeliest man to do any good. Why that wonderful detective has just been making fools of us!"

"Mr. Egerton promised to write again soon, when he had anything to tell. Mr. Standish may have a letter any day."

"Perhaps he has, to-day. I fancy he has come, too, for I heard the door-bell a few minutes ago."

"Miss Oakeley is in the drawing-room," said Dorothy, without stirring.

"I wish the Colonel was back, Miss Dorothy. He'll be wandering about over the old places and to that lonely little churchyard, breaking his heart, if that can be done twice over. That's where he used to go every time he went out, before he went away with Mr. Egerton. Many a time I've heard the front door open softly, and got up to watch him steal out in the grey of the morning."

"How do you know he went there, Nurse?"

"Because he always took the Rookstone road, and you'll remember a bit of a boy that used to bring us new-laid eggs sometimes? Well, he told me how he had been herding sheep on the hill-side behind the little chapel, and saw the poor gentleman in the early morning once stooping down and gathering the heather there and laying himself down on the ground in his grief."

"Ah, what he must have suffered, and how wonderfully he controls himself in our sight!"

"True for you, Miss Dorothy."

"You never mentioned this before, Nurse."

"No; why should I? Hadn't you enough to distract you? But I wish that decent, sensible man, Collins, had gone with him. He'll be terrible lonesome. Come now, my dears, I must clear that table, and get tea. Let Miss Dorothy go; she is wanted downstairs."

"And when you have finished tea, you shall come down too," said Dorothy, escaping with some difficulty.

Descending slowly, Dorothy found the drawing-room door ajar, and, entering softly, saw Henrietta and Standish in the recess formed by a bay window; their backs were to her. He held Henrietta's hand, and as Dorothy paused, uncertain as to her next movement, Standish exclaimed warmly, "My dear Henrietta, how can I ever thank you enough?" and kissed the hand he held.

Dorothy slipped away as noiselessly as she had entered, and went down to a small study, where she selected a book; then, feeling strangely tremulous, she sat down and tried to clear her thoughts from the painful haze which seemed to dim them. Soon, very soon it seemed to her, Collins came in and said, "Miss Oakeley desired me to say that tea is ready, Miss."

"Very well; I will come."

The cosy tea-table was set close by the fire; Henrietta held the teapot, and Standish stood on the rug.

"Where have you been, Dorothy?" cried the tea-maker. "I have sent up and down to find you. Mr. Standish has a letter from Mr. Egerton, he wanted to show you."

"There is very little in it," said Standish. He had shaken hands with his ward, looking kindly and anxiously into her face, and then drawn over a chair for her.

"I never expected much from him," returned Dorothy.

"He certainly is not sparing himself," returned Standish. "Here is his letter." Dorothy took it and laid it on the table.

Standish watched her with some curiosity, and Henrietta, who seemed in high spirits, launched into a description of her Aunt Callander's unreasonableness about the children, about of the trouble they gave when they did go to see her, and the terribly bad system on which they were brought up.

Then, looking at her watch, she exclaimed: "Oh, I must go out! I promised

my aunt to see her to-day. She has a bad
cold. Indeed, I do not think she is at all
well. I am quite sorry about her, poor
old thing! You can tell Dorothy what we
have been talking about, Mr. Standish.
Ring the bell, please, and tell Collins to
get me a cab. Good-bye," she added to
Standish, "I suppose you will be gone by
the time I come back."

As soon as they were alone, Standish,
after looking very earnestly at Dorothy,
sat down on the sofa behind her.

"Don't you care to read the letter?"
he asked.

"I should prefer hearing its contents
from you?"

Her voice sounded dull and despondent.

"Well then," taking it up, "Egerton,
after much searching, has found an old
muleteer whose nephew, Pedro, is a sailor,
and was, the old man thinks, on board a

vessel that traded between Cadiz and the Levant, and sometimes went further. The muleteer does not know where he is now, but he appeared last December at Alicant, and seemed very flush of cash. Since then he has gone to sea again, and his return is problematical."

"Yes, I suppose it is—very," returned Dorothy quietly.

"My dear Dorothy, something is working in your mind which you hide from me. It is tormenting and distressing you. Don't you think you had better open your heart to me?"

As he spoke, Collins came in to clear away the tea-things, and until he was gone neither of them spoke.

Then Standish repeated: "Don't you think so, Dorothy?"

"No, Paul. It would be of no use. In fact I have ceased to look back; all I care for now is to win poor Herbert back to something like his old self."

" Well, Dorothy, I cannot force you to speak if you do not choose to do so. But what have I done that you shut up your heart from me ? You have shrunk from all our old confidential communications. Have I slipped out of my former place in your esteem ? Eh, Dorothy ? "

Her heart swelled with an intense long-ing to throw her arms round his neck, as she used when in former years she flew to him with any childish complaint against her teachers ; but, with a remarkable effort of self-control, she smiled sweetly in his face, and said, a little unsteadily ;

" Dear Paul ! as if I could ever change to you, my best friend ! I shall have heaps of confidences to pour into your sympa-thetic ear from time to time, if you have patience to hear them ! "

She held out her hand in her old, frank
way.   Standish held it for a moment between his own, looking very grave.

"I am always ready to listen to you,
dear Dorothy, and wish you would trust
me for your own sake."

"What is it Henrietta told you to tell
me?"

"We have been arranging a scheme for
Callander and all of you.   We propose
that when the time for which you took this
house is up—that is in about a fortnight, I
think—you should set up your headquarters in Brussels.   There are pictures, and
churches, and the field of Waterloo for
Callander to meditate upon, and you are *en
route* everywhere.   Henrietta, I mean Miss
Oakeley, thinks that if you persuade Callander that you cannot travel without him,
he will consent to live with you, and then,
the children and yourselves being constantly

with him, will draw him gradually out of himself. He has sent in his papers and gives up the army, I am sorry to say, though I quite expected it."

" Yes! Oh, he could hardly go back to the regiment. I think the idea of getting him away to a totally different life is very good. If he will only agree to the plan! I do wish he was all right with you! It will be trying to Henrietta if you cannot go and come as you used."

" To Henrietta! Yes, and to me, too; and, pray, don't *you* care to see me any more?"

The question was put playfully, but, strive as she would, Dorothy could not respond in the same tone.

" Not wish to see you?" she repeated, with quivering lips, while her eyes filled up with sudden tears: " What should I do without you ?"

"My dear little Dorothy," exclaimed Standish, sitting down by her on the sofa, and putting his arm round her, he tried to draw her close to him.

But Dorothy struggled to free herself with an impetuosity which amazed him, and he immediately let her go.

"I beg you a thousand pardons for forgetting you are a grand, grown-up young lady," he said, with a novel sense of awkwardness. "You see, I used to be so accustomed to kiss away your tears, that I was on the point of repeating the panacea. If you but knew how it pains me to see your pale, sad face, you would not be vexed by my lapse of good manners."

"Vexed! oh, no; not vexed!" murmured Dorothy, confusedly. Then, in a tone of relief: "Here are the children!"

Dolly and "Boy" were warmly welcomed.

Standish gave the latter endless rides on his foot, and let Dolly clamber about him, take out his watch, re-arrange his chain, and generally do what she liked.

In the intervals of these amusements, he contrived to ask Dorothy what she had been reading, to recommend her some books, and offer to send them to her; to ask her if she had summoned courage to touch the piano once more, and to beg her to make the effort to resume her old way of life. But there was an undefinable change in his tone. He seemed suddenly to have gone a long way off.

At last he was obliged to leave. He had barely left himself time to dress for dinner.

"Then you like and approve of our Brussels scheme?" he said.

"Yes. I think it is the best thing to be done."

38*

"Then you can discuss it with Henrietta this evening and I shall see you to-morrow, when I hope there will be some tidings of Callander. Good evening, my dear ward."

A noisy farewell from the children, and he was gone.

"Why did he kiss Henrietta's hand? and what was it he thanked her for so enthusiastically?"

She went to sleep with this unanswered question preying on her heart.

CHAPTER III.

THEY—that is, Mrs. Callander, Henrietta and Dorothy—waited in vain for a letter from the Colonel.

A week had passed, and he made no sign. Dorothy was very uneasy, much more so than Henrietta or his mother, neither of whom shared her profound foreboding of evil. To them, his abstraction, his indifference to all that formerly interested him, the distressed expression of his eyes, sometimes so dull, sometimes wild and restless, were only marks of natural but unusually deep grief. To Dorothy they were indications of mental anguish too strong for the control of reason.

She had written more than one letter to

the hotel at Fordsea where she believed Callander had put up, but he took no notice of them.

It was, therefore, with a sense of infinite relief she heard Collins tap at the door, as she was changing her warm out-door dress for one of lighter material, and say, in a brisk, cheerful tone :

"If you please, miss, the Colonel has come. He is in the drawing-room, and I am going to bring Miss Dolly and Master Bertie."

"Yes, do, Collins. I will come directly. Oh! thank God!" she ejaculated to herself, and hastened to finish dressing.

Callander was sitting by the fire in a large arm-chair, his hand on Dolly's head. Both children were standing by him most demurely, gazing with wondering awed eyes at their now half-forgotten father. All seemed silent.

"Dear Herbert, I am so delighted to see you!" cried Dorothy, running to greet and embrace him. He smiled absently, and stretched out his hand to her. "Why did you not write? I felt so anxious about you."

"I was quite well. I had nothing to write about. Where is Henrietta?"

"She has gone to spend the afternoon and dine with some friends who are passing through on their way to Algeria. But you will dine with me, will you not?"

"Yes. I came here for my dinner."

"Don't you find the children looking well? Boy has quite recovered his looks and strength."

Callander looked earnestly at little Dolly, and suddenly lifting her, hugged her close to his breast and smothered her with kisses, till the child, half-frightened, struggled to get down.

"Me too — me too!" cried the boy, eager, as usual, to be noticed. Callander took him up more soberly, and kissed him.

"How old is the little fellow?" he asked, in a dreamy voice.

"Nearly two years. Is he not a big boy?" Callander did not reply. He let the child tug at his chain.

But Dolly, with some vague instinct of pity, nestled close to her father, and taking his hand, which hung listlessly down, put it round her neck.

"My little darling!" he said softly, in a tone more like his old natural voice than Dorothy had heard for some time. The next moment he said to her, almost in a whisper:

"Send them away, Dorothy — do send them away!"

The children were not particularly

reluctant to retire when Mrs. McHugh appeared, and said good night demurely.

The *tête-à-tête* which ensued was very trying. Callander sat quite still, answering the observations she forced herself to make from time to time with monosyllables, or the briefest possible sentences. She thought dinner would never be announced. When, at length, they were at table, she was surprised at her brother-in-law's voracious appetite. Collins waited on him with evident delight, no doubt thinking that nothing can be far wrong when a man can take his meals heartily. It increased Dorothy's uneasiness to observe how utterly oblivious Callander was of all the little attentions he used to pay his *convives* with such kindly politeness. He was absorbed in what he was eating, and drank eagerly the claret-and-water supplied him by his watchful attendant.

How Dorothy longed for Standish! She was growing nervous—foolishly nervous.

When they returned to the drawing-room, Callander again took the large easy chair, Dorothy began some needlework, and sat opposite him, in token of her readiness to converse, if he was so inclined. He kept silence so long that Dorothy thought he was asleep.

Suddenly he sat upright and exclaimed, " You are not like her, and yet you are. You haven't her beauty!"

"I know that well, Herbert," she returned, hoping he would relieve his mind by talking of the dear dead.

" Still, she looks out of your eyes at me sometimes, Dorothy, and then I don't know whether I hate or love you! You used to be like a daughter to me, and you are a good, kind girl. You must always take care of those poor children!"

"Yes, I will, to the best of my ability," said Dorothy, with difficulty keeping back her tears.

"You must never let my mother get hold of them, mind that."

"I hope you will stay with them, and order what is to be done for them. As to Mrs. Callander, why are you so unkind to her? She is very unhappy."

"Because I cannot forget how unkind *she* was to my lost darling," he returned, sternly. "And you should not forget it either! I can never forgive her. And she wants to make out that I am weak—weak in brain! She sent that fellow, Dillon, to dog my steps down at Fordsea!"

"Indeed, I am sure she did not. He often goes down to Eastport in his endless search for traces of — of ——" she hesitated.

"Of the murderer," added Callander, with composure. "Ay, he may search, but *I*—I alone must punish, I tell you. I may wait, but I will have my revenge—by my own hand!"

Dorothy felt uneasy, but she wisely avoided contradicting him, and so kept silence. Callander, now fully roused, stood up and began to pace the room.

"What has Egerton been doing? Has he written?"

"Yes — he thinks he has found some traces."

"Ha, ha, ha!" laughed Callander—rather a terrible laugh. "He will never find the murderer away there!—never!" And he paused opposite her.

"At all events, he said, in his letter to Paul Standish——"

"Standish!" repeated Callander, with a deadly, bitter tone, that made the word sound like a curse. "Why do you speak his name to me? I wonder you dare!" And he resumed his restless walk. This seemed to Dorothy an opportunity for asking an explanation of his mysterious dislike to her guardian.

"I do not know why I should not name him, Herbert. Tell me why you dislike him. It might relieve your mind."

"Tell you?" he repeated, "tell you? I have sometimes wished to tell you, that you might know what a subtle devil——" He broke off, and muttered some thing to him self. "There," he resumed, "you loved her well. You would shield her memory well."

"I would do anything for her sake— anything to comfort *you!*" cried poor Dorothy, unable to restrain her tears.

Callander paced the room in silence for another minute, then he suddenly sat down

by her on the sofa, which was her usual
seat, and, taking both her hands, which he
held tightly, he said, low and quick: "I
will tell you all—all! I found it out
before — just before — we lost her. It was
my mother pointed it out! But before that,
before I left India—there was a change, a
faint change, in her letters. *You* would
not have seen it — no one would have seen
it but a lover such as I was! I felt and
knew that something had come between
us" Dorothy sat listening, motionless, with
curdling blood.   Had he indeed discovered
the truth ?

"My mother wrote that Standish almost
lived with her and you, but I would not
notice her insinuations. Then I came
home, and I knew there *was* a change.
Still, she had some love for me, but *he* was
always at her ear! He would not let her
come away with me alone! That would

have made all right. So I determined to have his life; but she — she ——" His voice failed him, and he paused, panting, big drops standing on his brow.

" Paul Standish!" cried Dorothy, wrenching her hands from him, all her force and courage returning, " Paul Standish is as innocent as I am. What—who put this horrible idea into your head? You did not believe your mother, who told you this horrible lie?"

" It is no lie!" he said, with a moan like that of a creature in pain. "I saw it in her own writing."

" She never wrote anything to Paul Standish which the whole world might not see. Who has imposed upon you?"

" Ah! you do not know. Neither she nor he would speak of such evil things to *you*. But, Dorothy, I will have patience, subtilty as profound as his, *and* patience.

I will punish him yet, cruelly, unrelent-
ingly. God! I feel my hand on his throat
now!" and he clenched both his own,
looking awfully wild, the fine strong face
she knew so well distorted by passion to
a demon-like expression.

Dorothy felt as if Paul's doom was fixed,
that nothing could save him. She—she
only could undeceive the wretched man
before her.

"You are wrong, Herbert!" she said,
bravely and steadily. "I can prove that
you are wrong; I can prove that Mabel
always loved you, that you do Paul Standish
the greatest injustice. Will you wait here
for a few minutes, and will you read what I
bring you?"

Callander, checked and astonished by
her words and impressive manner, stopped,
silent and still. "What do you mean?"
he stammered.

"You shall see!" she cried, and flew away upstairs to where, in the secret drawer of her old dressing-case, enclosed in a blank envelope, lay the letter she had never been able to deliver into Egerton's hands. All fear, all hesitation was gone. What matter any danger to herself from the fury of the excited man she had left behind? What matter the desperate retribution she might bring down on the real offender? Everything was secondary to the desire of proving that Mabel was really true to her husband, that Standish was innocent of the hideous treachery attributed to him—all consequences were swallowed up in this overpowering motive.

Almost breathless she returned to the drawing-room. Callander was standing exactly where she had left him.

He stretched out his hand eagerly.

"One moment, Herbert! there are one

or two things to tell first." Rapidly, yet
with a prudence which was almost inspiration, she told of the curious mesmeric
power which Egerton had gained over her
sister, of her dread that Callander might
be suspicious, of Mabel's confession of her
unhappiness and fear of Egerton's violence
should she show affection to her husband.
" Then she determined to end this wretched,
contemptible state of things, and wrote
this, which I was to give to *him*, but I
never had a chance, for she died dreadfully
a few days after." She took the note from
its outer cover, and gave it to Callander.
He took it, and looked curiously at the
address with dilated, horror-struck eyes.
His hands trembled while he tore it open.
She watched him eagerly as he read the
contents, every word of which was engraven
on her memory — all fear, all personal
feeling, lost in the intense desire to clear

the two creatures she loved best from the terrible accusation in which Callander believed.

" I cannot bear my life," so ran the letter, " if you continue to exercise the extraordinary power I have let you gain over me. I told you this before in the last lines I wrote. Now I will break my fetters, and dare to act as my heart and conscience dictate. My husband loves me; in spite of all you say, I believe he loves me, and I really love him. I only *fear* you, Randal, and I cannot understand how you gained the power over me which you have. I am determined to resist it. If you ever cared for me, if you have any principle, any sense of honour, leave me to regain peace and happiness. You can never persuade me to leave my dear, good husband. I shudder to think I ever listened to you

for a moment. Show that you have some
real regard for me by going far away, and
earn the gratitude of

"M. C."

Callander's chest heaved. He drew his
breath in gasps. When he came to the
end, he looked up with wild, angry eyes,
and crushing the paper in his hand, said,
in fierce, quick tones : " Egerton was your
lover—he wanted to marry *you !* "

" He pretended it ! "

" Oh, my God ! " exclaimed Callander,
in a tone of anguish that thrilled Dorothy's
heart, and he dropped into a chair as if
shot, sitting upright, motionless, like a
creature turned to stone.

Dorothy was terrified at the effect of her
confession.   What should she do ?

" Oh, Herbert ! speak to me."

He stared at her as if not understanding

what she said, and covered his face with his hands, leaning forward until his brow almost touched his knees. Then he stood up, began smoothing out the letter, and kissed it. "She loved me," he said brokenly —"she loved me still. I cannot speak to you, my poor child. I must go. I dare not speak. To-morrow—to-morrow!" He staggered towards the door.

"Oh, Herbert! Let me call Collins to go with you; you are not fit to be alone, dear Herbert." He made a motion of refusal with his hand.

"At least you see that Paul Standish is not to blame."

"I have wronged him, but I will write. Let me go! for God's sake, let me go!" He rushed from the room.

Dorothy rang violently and then ran downstairs.

"Oh, Collins, get your hat and follow

him, there is something dreadful in his
face!" and Collins flew to obey her.

"Have I done right or wrong?" asked
Dorothy of herself, while she wrung her
hands in despair. "What shall I do?
Where can I turn? Oh, I must tell Paul
everything. What will Herbert say or do
when he has time to think, and connects
this letter with the awful result? I did
so hope to keep all a secret, for my poor
darling's sake. Will he attack Randal
Egerton legally, and blazon out the whole
dreadful story? I must see Paul, and he will
be out now. It is nearly nine o'clock. He
will be away, goodness knows where. Still,
Henrietta is safe away; it will be eleven
or more before she returns. Perhaps Paul
may be at his rooms. I will go to him.
I don't want to tell Henrietta more than I
can help; but I must tell someone. Nurse
will not say a word if I ask her," and

she mounted rapidly to the peaceful nursery, where Mrs. McHugh, spectacles on nose, was reading a newspaper with a stern aspect, as if sitting in judgment on the world. "Dear Nurse, the Colonel has just rushed out of the house in such a state of excitement that I am frightened to death."

"What's put him out?" asked Mrs. McHugh, rising.

"We were talking of—of the past, and he spoke of Mabel, almost for the first time since we lost her, and got into a state of despair! I have sent Collins to try and find him. Now I want to see Mr. Standish. Oh! Nurse, I must see him at once, I am going to him. Will you get a cab for me? I must go."

"Stay a bit, Miss Dorothy, it's just a chance if he be at home. You stay here, I'll go," beginning to take off her cap as

she spoke   "I'll bring him back if he is
to be found.   You write a line for me to
leave."

"But, Nurse, I don't want Miss Oakeley
to know."

"All right, Miss Dorothy, more reason I
should go. No one will tell on me, but
Brown " (the lady's maid) " would be sure
to say you had gone out by yourself—go
write, my dear young lady."

"I will, and I will watch the children.
You need not send Peggy up."

A short appeal to Standish to come to
her early next day, at eight if he liked,
was quickly penned, and then there was
nothing for it but to wait.

"Nothing but to wait!" What a terrible
task, to be still and helpless while others are
casting the shuttle of your life through the
threads of inexorable circumstance. To
count the leaden moments and wear out

thought, striving to forecast the turn of the tide in your affairs !—to divine the " trifles light as air," which may influence the decision of some all potent friend or patron for or against the aim of your existence, the desire of your heart—to wait while another pleads your cause, while the " yes " or " no " which will make or mar you depends on no effort of your own. This is perhaps the most severe test to which human courage and endurance can be put. The pluck of ordinary men can carry them gallantly through the excitement of a dashing charge —when motion gives fire to the blood and action disguises the individual's danger— but to those who can stand still and firm to bear the shock of the onset they see coming against them, these are the true heroes.

True, Dorothy was quite certain that Standish would come to her as soon as he possibly could, but what would he say to the tale she had to tell? Had she done right in giving that letter to Callander? Yes. The more she reflected, the more satisfied she became that it was right to undeceive him.

How slowly the minutes went by! She sat watching the hands of the clock on the mantelpiece. Did time ever drive so slowly? She took up the newspaper Mrs McHugh had thrown down, it was a weekly paper, brim-full of horrors, murders, maimings of wives by their husbands, vitriol-throwing by wives over husbands and rivals, fights, suicides—this last was a terribly suggestive item. When? When would Collins come back? She laid down the paper and glanced again at the clock. Even that very temporary occupation had helped her over many minutes.

At last steps approached, the door

opened and Mrs. McHugh appeared, a little breathless.

"Well, I've been pretty quick, haven't I? But I am vexed, he was out. He had gone down with Lord R—— to some place down the Great Northern line, and won't be home till to-morrow evening."

Dorothy uttered a faint cry, and sank into a chair.

"Don't take on so, my dear! I just got his address and sent on your note."

"Thank you, Nurse! but he will not get it till mid-day in the country. I must telegraph the first thing in the morning, that is all I can do."

"I suppose so! Write the telegram then, Miss Dorothy. I'll see it goes as soon as the office is open. Hasn't Collins come back?"

Dorothy shook her head.

"Dear, dear, that's bad."

"Yes, very bad, I fear."

"I'll go down and watch for him, and send Peggy up. It's time she went to bed."

"I think I will go and wait for him in the drawing-room," said Dorothy, faintly. "I do hope he will come in before Henrietta."

This seemed a little strange to Nurse, but she made no remark upon it.

Dorothy went to get a telegraph form, and wrote an entreaty to Standish to return at once.

"Don't go to bed till I come and tell you what news Collins brings," she said to Mrs. McHugh.

"You may be sure I will not."

Then she went away to "wait" again.

This time she was not long left alone —a little before eleven Miss Oakeley returned.

" Why, where in the world is Collins?"
were her first words, " and—good Heavens,
Dorothy, what is the matter with you?
you look ghastly!"

Dorothy gave the same explanation she
had offered to Nurse.

"What a dreadful business! My dear
child, he is as likely to throw himself into
the river as to go to his hotel! What in
the world did you say to him to drive him
into such a state?"

"Oh! it was talking and thinking of
the past, that upset him. Henrietta, you
terrify me."

" I am afraid you were not very prudent,
but don't tremble so, I did not mean to
frighten you. You had better go to bed,
you poor little soul."

"Ah, no, Henrietta, not till I see
Collins."

" I will go and put on my dressing-gown—I wonder when that man will come back!"

Dorothy sat with her head on her hand, her lips moving in silent prayer, she had stirred and risen up to seek Henrietta, unable to endure the solitude, when to her relief Collins presented himself.

A glance at his face showed her that he had no evil tidings.

"I've had a rare hunt, Miss Dorothy," were his first words. "When I got out of the door——"

"Oh, good gracious, Collins! is he safe?" cried Miss Oakeley, coming in as he spoke

"Yes'm, he's all right. I was a sayin', as I got out of the door I felt I was too late. I couldn't see a sign of him. Maybe he's gone to Kensington Gardens, thinks I so I went there as fast as my legs could carry me, but as I saw nothing on the way

a bit like him, I thought there'd be no end
of looking for him under those dark trees,
so I returned the other way towards town
and got to the hotel! No sign of him! So I
went back and up and down, and to and
fro, all to no good. At last I went to the
hotel once more, and there he was all right,
just come in, and the waiter was going to
take him a brandy and soda—so I made
bold to go up, and asked if he had any
commands for me to-morrow. He was
lying back, dead beat like, in his chair, and
as the man picked up his boots to take
them away, I saw there was some mould
and grass sticking to the soles. He didn't
take much notice of me, but presently
he rose up and bid me give him his
dressing-gown, and as I helped him
off with his coat I saw that the back
and one side was all marked with grass
and mould, as if he had lain on the

ground, yet he didn't look as if he had had a fit."

"A fit! What a notion, Collins!" cried Miss Oakeley. "Did he say he would go to bed?"

"He didn't say nothing, ma'am, except, when I asked, he said I might come round in the morning, and I'm going early—and if you please, I met Mr. Dillon coming out, and he has been down at Fordsea. He heard something as took him there, and he saw the Colonel once or twice. He says, Miss, as the Colonel would kill himself if he were let go on the way he did. He used to go out bathing in this sharp, cold weather! — out in a boat, so far as I can make out, with the old boatman as used to row Mrs. McHugh and the children last summer— sometimes he went with him, and sometimes without; but he was always saying it was hot, and how it set him up to have a dip."

" How extraordinary!" cried Dorothy.

" How dreadfully imprudent!" said Henrietta.

" Any ways, Mr. Dillon had been talking with the old boatman—and he said as how the Colonel was as nice and liberal a gentleman as ever, but that quiet and silent!—may be, the salt water didn't do him no good. Mr. Dillon wanted to know when Mr. Standish would be back. He'd been to his rooms, and he was out of town!"

" That is very provoking!" said Henrietta. "How I wish the Colonel would make up with him!" Dorothy frowned at her slightly as a warning to be prudent, and said: " You must be tired, Collins— you had better have some supper, and go to bed!"

"Thank you, Miss! I will—and if you don't mind my waiting at breakfast, I'll go round early to the Colonel."

"Oh, yes, pray do!" exclaimed Miss Oakeley.

"Thank God he seems all right," she continued when they were alone. "Brandy and soda sounds like sanity."

"Will he ever be himself again?" asked Dorothy, with a deep sigh.

"Yes! I think he will," returned Henrietta thoughtfully. "Men always recover. Now that we know he is safe, let us go to bed; I am most dreadfully tired. How I wish Paul Standish was not away!"

"So do I. In fact he must come back; I shall telegraph for him the first thing to-morrow morning," said Dorothy decidedly.

"I am sure you are right! I shall be so glad to see him!"

"But Henrietta!" began Dorothy,

hesitatingly, and nerving herself to secure a *tête-à-tête* with Standish, which she felt to be indispensable, "I hope you will not think me unfriendly or unkind, but I must see Paul alone."

"Good gracious! Why?"

"Because I must tell him some things—Oh, some things that Herbert said to me about Paul in confidence, which I hope will make them friends again!"

"And don't you suppose they would both tell *me* as soon as they would you?"

"Oh, very likely!—only for the present I want to say my say to Paul Standish alone. You know I have been accustomed to tell him everything from a child."

"Oh, very well!—but of course he will pass it all on to me. I suppose he cannot be here much before two! I'll go over and lunch with my aunt, who does not seem to get over her cold; and no doubt

40*

when I return, you will tell me everything."

"Perhaps so," said Dorothy, anxious to
escape from the subject; but above all,
desirous to secure a private interview with
Standish.

Still quivering with the strain and terror
of the last three hours, the question which
last occupied her thoughts, above even her
deep anxiety about her unhappy brother-
in-law, was: "Can Paul Standish really
confide every thought of his heart to Henrietta? Kind and true as she is there
is a crude realism about her that makes
her take such matter-of-fact views about
everything!"

Fatigued by emotion, she at last dropped
asleep, with this query unanswered.

CHAPTER IV.

"THE PLOT THICKENS."

WHAT a long morning it was!

Henrietta kept her promise, and went away to Mrs. Callander, having waited for a report of the Colonel from Collins. He seemed as usual, but said he had a cold, and would not leave the house. He had made Collins put out his writing materials, and said he had much to do.

"I think I shall go and see him," were Henrietta's last words. "I will talk to my aunt about it.

Dorothy went through the form of luncheon, but could hardly swallow; and then retreated into the study—the room she considered the most safe from intrusion

It was nearly three o'clock, surely he might have come by this time? She had just turned from putting some fresh coal on the fire when the door was hastily opened, and Standish came in un-announced.

She flew to him with outstretched hands.

" Oh! thank God you are come."

" Dear Dorothy! what is the trouble?" He drew her to him, and pressed her hands against his heart.

" I have a long, long story to tell! I almost dread to hear your judgment, Paul; I acted on impulse, but——"

" For God's sake, what is it? Have you promised to marry some one, and want my consent?"

" Marry? I marry? No!"

" Then let us sit down and talk."

" Don't you want something to eat, Paul?"

"No! I ate something at a detestable junction, where I was compelled to waste half-an-hour! Now, my own little Dorothy, you are my own *ward*, you know. Tell me everything—keep back nothing!"

He wheeled round an arm-chair for her and took his stand on the hearth-rug.

" First of all, I have found out the reason of Herbert's dislike to you, and removed it."

All her nervous terrors seemed to evaporate in his reassuring presence. The light of his kind grave eyes seemed to calm her.

"Ha! this is something! Go on!"

Then Dorothy began at the beginning, and described the conversation she had overheard between her sister and Egerton, her remonstrance with Mabel, the letter the latter had written, and left with Dorothy to deliver, how she had never found an opportunity to do so, how Mabel's cruel death seemed to have closed the account; that some instinct had kept her from destroying the letter, some vague idea of punishing Egerton had held her hand.

Then she described Callander's outburst the evening before, his extraordinary belief in Paul's treachery.

"I could not bear that," continued Dorothy. "If he had killed me I should have told him the truth; so I flew to get the letter I had kept, and gave it to him. He read it through—oh, Paul! how his poor hands trembled—and then he kissed it. The idea that she loved him through all seemed to please him. How he has suffered ! Surely death is scarce a grief, compared to the agony of losing the love of anyone *you* love ? " In the restlessness of strong emotion, Dorothy rose to her feet, she was trembling, and could hardly steady her voice.

Standish put his arm round her, and pressed her to him.

"This has been a cruel experience for you, Dorothy, too sore a trial for your young strength! But I scarcely know what to say to your desperate expedient of showing Callander that letter. In his frame of mind, it is almost death to Egerton. Think of all *that* entails."

"I do think. I have thought, Paul," she said, raising her eyes to his with a resolute look. "I do not regret what I have done. I have saved *you*. He would have killed *you*, then I should have lost both you *and* Herbert. I could never see him again if he had hurt you. What is Egerton's life to me? He deserves to die. But you, my best——" A blinding gush of tears choked her utterance, and she hid her face against his shoulder.

Standish pressed her closely to him, and

murmured some half articulate words of comfort. She felt his heart beating strongly against her own, and was conscious that she could stay in those dear arms for ever, half because of the weary child's desire to be comforted; half from the passionate woman's love for the man who had been everything to her from her childhood.

"Do you blame me, Paul?" she murmured, at length regaining her voice.

"Blame you!"—he paused, looking down on the small brown head leaning against him, and stroking back the wavy hair from her brow—"how could I blame you, dear? After all, it was only just to our poor Mabel to let her husband see the truth of her heart."

Dorothy made a slight effort to release herself, but Paul's close, gentle hold did not relax. "What an infernal villain Egerton has been!" he continued. "I should like to shoot him, myself! and we must not attack him! I must do my best to keep Callander quiet; the scandal of such a fracas would be too hideous to incur; even you can see the cruel construction the world would put on it."

"I do, Paul," she returned, extricating herself from him, and leaning against the back of her chair. "For poor Mabel's sake we must let her murderer go free."

"Her murderer?" he repeated. "What do you mean?"

"Do you not see that he was her murderer, either with his own hand or that of his emissary, the Spaniard?"

"My God, Dorothy! How do you come to suspect him of being such a monster?" exclaimed Standish, gazing at her amazed.

"Did I not tell you I heard him threaten to crush out her life if she preferred her husband to him, only a few days before her murder ? and she never saw him alone after."

"But you forget, he had not seen the letter avowing her intention of breaking with him."

"She had written before to the same effect, and he took no notice."

"Still, I never for a moment can believe that he, an English gentleman, would do so foul a deed!"

"*I* believe it. Look at his conduct, his extraordinary grief, his avoidance of us all."

"Conscience, remorse for the guilt he *had* incurred, might account."

"No, Paul. He *is* guilty. I had a stormy interview with him just before he went to Spain, when I accused him, wildly and incoherently enough ; and, though he denied it, he did so in a half-hearted way. Remember, his blood is not all English.

That unpleasant detective suspects him too. I understand his hints about the peculiar difficulties of the case. Oh, it is all too like a hideous nightmare. It has almost driven me wild to be obliged to see the base, cruel destroyer of my sweet sister."

"There is something queer about that fellow Dillon's mode of dealing with the case. Still, I cannot for a moment accept your theory. I wish you had not adopted it ; it must have added considerably to the horrors you have so bravely endured in silence. Dorothy, you are a true-hearted real woman, to have locked all this into your heart. I would trust my life with you. I shall never call you child or little Dorothy again. You have attained a mental stature that forbids either, only *my* dear Dorothy you will always be. He took and kissed her hand, holding it awhile.

"Right or wrong, guilty or not," he resumed, "I must keep Callander from encountering Egerton. Shall I go to see him? It will be an infinite relief to feel that he is all right with me again, shall I go?"

"I almost think you had better not; he sent word by Collins this morning that he has a great deal of writing to get through, and as he told me he was going to write to you, you had better wait for his letter. I feel it very hard, Paul, to see Mrs. Callander; she has embittered all our lives."

"She is a mischief-making, implacable she-devil!" cried Standish, with energy. "By Heaven, I don't think I shall ever speak to her again! Were it not for *you*, Dorothy, I should tax her with her infamous slander of myself."

"Do not mind me. I do not care to hold with her, except for Henrietta's sake.

And, Oh, Paul! Henrietta wants to know so much what I had to talk to you about. I would rather not tell her *all*"—hesitatingly.

"No; certainly not," promptly. "*I* will tell her that it was poor Callander's confession of his mother's insinuations against me, that you wished to explain. Leave it to me—and, Dorothy, I shall write to Egerton. I shall let him know that we fully understand the dastardly part he has played, and shall warn him that he has to reckon with Callander."

"Oh, leave him alone, Paul. He might murder *you*. Such a man is capable of anything."

"He is a villain, undoubtedly, but, my dear Dorothy, I absolve him from the crime of murder. That seems quite impossible! He is bad enough, but, good God! to kill a defenceless woman in her sleep! Besides, it would have punished himself——"

"Paul, I feel certain Mr. Dillon suspects him."

"There is something curious in Dillon's mode of proceeding, I grant; still, this conviction of yours is really only the result of excited nerves. I am surprised. You have too heavy a burden to bear, dear Dorothy. I wish I were sure of a reconciliation with Callander, I could then be of some use in reassuring your mind in one direction, at least. I wish I could take you away somewhere. A complete change of scene might restore the tone of your mind."

"I feel better already since I opened my heart to you, and if I know Herbert is with you and confides in you, I shall be much more at rest. But, oh! keep him and yourself from Egerton. He is capable of anything."

" Did you really tax him with this atrocious crime?" asked Paul, with some curiosity.

" I did, and he seemed startled and confused."

" He might be that, though innocent. Tell me, Dorothy; was it some instinct that he was playing a part which induced you to refuse him?"

" I think so, Paul."

" I confess that your rejection of so very attractive a person made me suspect that some luckier fellow had forestalled him."

" Why did you think so?" asked Dorothy, a sudden vivid blush dyeing her pale cheeks.

" Oh, I don't know. It was a surmise," returned Standish, slowly, while his eyes dwelt searchingly on her.

She heaved a deep sigh, and the colour faded from her cheek.

"I think I heard Henrietta come in. Will you see her alone, Paul? I do not think I could bear to talk any more to anyone."

"Go and lie down and rest then. I will see Henrietta and explain matters, as I said I would. Try and compose yourself. Remember I am always at your service. I wish I could do more for you, my sweet ward."

"Thank you. Good-bye for the present."

"I shall see you this evening, probably. I am not sure that I shall not go and see Callander. It might be some comfort to him, poor fellow."

*   *   *   *   *

Standish explained matters so much to Henrietta's satisfaction that she came to talk with Dorothy before dinner.

"You poor dear. Is your head any better? Well, you see Paul Standish was not long in telling me all about it. What an awful fury he is in with Aunt Callander. Indeed, I am not surprised at it. I somehow got used to her dislike and insinuations. She couldn't bear Paul, and was not too fond of poor dear Mabel; but I never thought the nonsense she talked would make such an impression on Herbert. It will be delightful if he makes friends with Mr. Standish again, and a great help. Oh, who do you think I saw to day in Bond Street? Major St. John! He stopped the carriage, and we had a talk. He is coming to see me to-morrow. He was looking so well—quite handsome, and seemed rather brighter than usual. He really would be quite creditable at the foot of one's table. To be sure, he is not one half so agreeable and amusing as Paul Standish, but then, again, Paul is rather contradictory and overbearing."

41*

"Have they had a lover's quarrel?"
thought Dorothy. "He has always been
very good to me," she said aloud.

"Oh, yes, I daresay; but then, of
course, he looks on you as a daughter.
Now I find him rather changeable. I am
very steady, myself, and I hate changeable,
whimsical people."

"Your temper is always steadily good,
Henrietta," said Dorothy. "I will get up
and do my hair now."

Standish came in the evening, and reported that he had called on Colonel
Callander, but he had gone out. On
enquiry, the hotel porter said he would
not return to dinner, and that he had
ordered the driver of the cab called for
him to drive to some number in Lincoln's
Inn Fields.

"That is Brierly's office—his solicitor,
you know—a very good fellow. If he

dines with him we could not desire anything better. Brierly is a bachelor and
has capital rooms in Victoria Street."

"Yes; that would be more like his old
self," said Henrietta, "only I wonder he
did not look you up. He will be quite
glad, I am sure, to be all right with you
again."

"I hope so. I daresay I shall have a
line from him to-morrow. He might like
to write a preliminary explanation before
meeting me."

For the rest of his stay Standish talked
cheerfully to Henrietta, and only at parting
asked, with an air of deep interest, if
Dorothy's head was free from pain now.

"I am afraid I shall not be able to see
you to-morrow," he said. "It will be a
busy day. I dine with Lord R——, too,
and go with him to the House of Commons."

"Pray, when are we to hail you as

ambassador extraordinary?" asked Henrietta. "That always seems to me such a
delicious sort of title."

"Not for many a day—if I ever reach so
high a position," said Standish, smiling,
and he wished them good-night.

The following day was altogether restful
to Dorothy. She felt safe after having
confided all the perilous stuff that had lain
heavy at her heart to Standish. His warm
sympathy was infinitely consoling. With
his help she did not despair of seeing her
brother-in-law restored to resignation and
composure. She, too, would try to
compose her nerves, and try to fulfil those
duties from which her dearly-loved sister
had been snatched.

Somehow or other she did not care to be
with Henrietta, good and kind as she was.
Dorothy felt that she jarred upon her in a
way she used not to do.

She therefore went out to walk with the children, and read a tough book in her own room, leaving Henrietta to entertain Major St. John by herself.

Collins on his return from his morning visit to his master reported him to be just as usual, but said the Colonel did not intend calling on the ladies till late.

"He will try and see Paul Standish first," they said to each other, when Collins left the room.

Now Standish had been a good deal exercised that morning by the receipt of a letter from Egerton.

The sight of the man's handwriting roused a degree of fury and indignation which quite upset his self-control for a few minutes.

Apart from the knowledge so lately imparted by Dorothy, Paul would have thought the letter a good one and full of kind sympathy—as it was, he read, between the lines, craft and hypocrisy. Perhaps, indeed Egerton might feel the sorrow he affected, for it was scarce possible that any conscience could be so seared as to be unmoved by the recollection of the devilish part he had played.

The letter was dated from Madrid, and stated that the writer had given up all hopes of tracing the man Pedro. Indeed there was a report in Valencia that a sailor answering to his description had been washed overboard a vessel plying to Tunis—in a storm off Cape Bon—"If this be the case one is naturally indignant that such a criminal should have slipped through the fingers of justice. But now it has got abroad that he is wanted, there is no doubt he will keep out of the way. I really think that Dillon mismanaged matters—so far as his search out here went—and I have grave doubts that he ever came here at all. I can find no trace of him, indeed his conduct all the way through has been suspicions. He is working some line of which we know nothing. I shall stay here about a week, and then go straight back to London, where I hope to find all brighter than when I left them."

Standish threw the letter from him in disgust, then he picked it up, and put it away carefully. There was no time to answer it, and it might perhaps be wiser not to express himself in writing on such compromising topics as would form the subject matter of a letter.

He was so infinitely revolted that he even thought, " Could Dorothy's woman-instinct be right, when she laid the crowning charge of murder against the refined, accomplished gentleman, who made so little of his duties, of friendship—of the obligations of a man of honour—what was there to hold him back from any felony which his evil, uncontrolled passions prompted ? "

While Standish, putting his private affairs out of his mind for the present, threw himself heartily into his work or discussed with his chief the political question on which the latter was to speak that evening, Henrietta Oakeley had spent on the whole a satisfactory day. She had bought several bargains quite "dirt cheap," and she had roused up the Hon. Major to some unusually strong expressions of admiration.

She was sitting with Dorothy in the drawing-room before dinner, and had just been expatiating on the dreariness of the first long days, and the evening light which is so cold at first, when Collins presented himself, and announced that Mrs. Callander's butler wished to speak to Miss Oakeley.

"Tell him to come up to me here," she exclaimed. "What is the matter now? What is it, Ransom?"

As the stately functionary came in and closed the door:

"If you please 'm—" he said with a loud "hem!" "Miss Boothby sent me round to ask if you would be so good as to come to Mrs. ·Callander, she is taken in rather a strange way! The Colonel, he paid her a visit this afternoon and stayed a good while 'm. He went away between four and five I think. I didn't let him out, for Mrs. Callander didn't ring the bell, but a while after, Miss Boothby went into the drawing-room and found the missis sitting stiff like in her chair, and the first thing she says was 'Get me some brandy and water,' which is what she never tastes, and then she ordered Miss Boothby to write for Mr. Greenwood the lawyer,

then she had the note torn up, next she
ordered that everything should be got
ready to start for Paris, after that she went
into a fit of hysterics and kept calling out
'my son, my son,' and she forbids us to
send for the doctor, and so Miss Boothby
would be ever so much obliged if you
would come to her, miss."

"Very well, Ransom. Call a cab and
I will go with you. Good gracious!" she
exclaimed, " she has had a tremendous row
with Herbert. He has been reproaching
her, and, though she richly deserves it,
I can't help being sorry for her! I declare I don't think we shall ever have a
peaceful hour again. I am getting sick
of it all."

When Henrietta reached Somerset Square,
an evident degree of disorganisation had
replaced the clock-work regularity of that
patent particular household. The cook

opened the door and the page might be perceived carrying a hot bottle upstairs.

"I'm sure, ma'am, Miss Boothby will be that thankful to see you."

"Where is she?"

"Upstairs, packing, 'm. Mrs. Callander has had the big trunks dusted and taken down, she says her feet are cold and her head burning."

Henrietta began to ascend the stair; half way up she met Miss Boothby with a distressed, bewildered expression.

"Oh! dear me, *I am* glad to see you, Miss Oakeley. I don't know what has come to Mrs. Callander. She doesn't know I sent for you."

"Very well. Let her think I came by accident."

She found Mrs. Callander walking to and fro in her bed-room, with a scent bottle in her trembling hand, her usually cold grey face much flushed and a strange frightened look in her eyes.

" Why, my dear Aunt! what has happened ?　Where are you going ? "

" Oh ! Henrietta," in a high nervous key. " I am tired of the constant cold and headaches from which I have suffered ! Really the climate of London is horrible, so I am just going off to Paris.　There is no reason why I should not go where I like.　I had rather a curious dizzy turn to-day, but I will not have the doctor, mind !　I will not see him if you *do* send for him ! "

" Well, I am sure you ought, aunt. You seem to me very unwell."

" You know nothing about it !　Go, Evans—Go, Miss Boothby—I wish to speak with my niece."

She sank into a chair as she spoke, and trembled visibly all over.

"Now then, aunt, what is it?" asked Henrietta peremptorily, when she had closed the door.

"I had a long and painful interview with my son," began Mrs. Callander, speaking in distressful gasps. "He behaved in an extraordinary manner, accused me of slandering his unfortunate wife, and said he would never see my face again!—And I have only lived for him."

"Men are generally ungrateful," said Miss Oakeley, easily. "But I thought better of Herbert. Still, he has been very sorely tried; you must have patience, and keep friends with him."

"It does not depend on me," returned Mrs Callander, and she shuddered visibly. "Have you seen my son since he was here this morning?"

"No; but he is coming to us, I believe, this evening."

"This evening! Oh, my heart! It beats so fast, and then stands still! Go away, Henrietta—you can do me no good! I only want to get away!"

"But, aunt, you are not fit to travel. Do see Dr. Birch, he will give you some soothing medicine. You are quite in a fever. Do send for him."

"Don't tell me what I am to do. I do not want you, Henrietta. I shall go to Meurice's, and don't tell anyone I am going away—I don't want people to talk about me."

"Well, aunt, I am quite uneasy about you."

"You need not trouble. I am most unfortunate! I——"

She burst into a violent fit of weeping, in the midst of which her maid announced that the Reverend Mr. Gilmore was down stairs, and wished to see her. Mrs. Callander paused in her weeping.

"I can't see him. I don't wish to see him," she exclaimed, angrily. "I will not be intruded on, or pried into. He may go away! I am particularly engaged."

Henrietta was infinitely amazed. She could hardly believe her ears when she heard her aunt refuse to admit one of her favourite preachers. Was the sky going to fall?

Then the greatly disturbed woman rose from her seat; and exclaiming: "I want to be alone—I want no one's help!" tottered into the bed-room adjoining her dressing-room, and emphatically closed the door.

"What can be the matter with her, Miss Boothby?" asked Henrietta, greatly perplexed.

"I am sure, Miss Oakeley, I can form no idea, except that she had some words with Colonel Callander. Really there seems no filial affection or respect left in the world!"

"I never saw her in such an extraordinary state before. There is no use in my staying here. You will let me know if she asks for me? I don't suppose for a moment that she will carry out her whim of going to Paris."

"It is impossible to say—but I'll let you know, Miss Oakeley. Nothing could wel be more inconvenient than to start off to the Continent just now. I thought we were safe to remain here to the end of the season."

"I don't think she will go. Pray don't leave her alone. I feel most uneasy about her."

Henrietta was not sorry to get out of the house.

"My dear Dorothy," she exclaimed, as

soon as she found herself safe in her own drawing-room, "Herbert has been driving his mother fairly out of her wits. I never thought anything in the world would put her into such a state."

"I wonder if he will say anything to us this evening, if he comes?" returned Dorothy.

But the hours sped on ; bed-time came, and no Callander appeared.

CHAPTER V.

"THE DETECTIVE'S STORY."

THE day described in the last chapter was a very busy one to Standish, but in the late afternoon he managed to call on Callander.

Standish was a good deal annoyed to hear that he had gone out of Town for a couple of days—where, the waiter did not know. Neither porter nor clerk could give him any information; only Boots knew that the direction given to the driver of the cab called for him was to Victoria.

Standish mused over Callander's possible reasons for choosing that route. He did not know of any which recommended it, for it was not likely he would visit either of the friends who resided near the lines converging at that station—True, Eastport and Fordsea could be reached by the South Coast Line ; but why should he not travel as usual by the South Eastern from Waterloo ?

Arriving at his chambers only in time to dress for dinner, Standish was a good deal disturbed by a letter which awaited him from Dillon.

" Sir," it ran ; " I should feel much obliged by your fixing some time most convenient to yourself, when you can give me an uninterrupted interview. I have now completed the search you commis· sioned me to make, and I am anxious to lay the results before you. You can then judge what claim I have to the reward offered by the relatives of the late Mrs.

Callander for the discovery of her assassin.
May I ask you to keep this communication
strictly private for the present?

"I am, yours respectfully,

"LUKE DILLON."

After a few minutes' thought, Standish
wrote a few lines, appointing the following
evening at eight o'clock.

The dinner to which he was engaged
proved very agreeable in every way. It
was a small gathering of men occupied in
politics, and the conversation was interesting, especially to Standish, to whom everything relating to England's foreign relations
was of the highest importance. But across
the intellectual excitement of interchanging
views and ideas with men of thought and
information came at intervals the stinging
question: "What is Dillon going to
reveal? Can it be possible that he

will verify Dorothy's wild conjecture, or rather her conviction? No, the idea is too outrageous."

It was a wild, stormy evening when Standish, having despatched a solitary meal at his club, returned to his own abode to await the appearance of Dillon.

He had not called at Princes Place, for he had an unaccountable reluctance to tell Dorothy of his expected interview, and he knew that Henrietta would worry him to stay to dinner.

He had had a note from her in the morning, describing her aunt's nervous seizure, and asking if he knew that Colonel Callander had gone out of town again. This he answered, promising to visit her the next day.

"Not at home to anyone except Mr. Dillon," was Paul's order to his servant as he exchanged his frock-coat for a smoking-jacket, and, lighting a cigar, took up an evening paper, to which he could not force himself to pay any attention. He had not long to wait. A few minutes after eight Dillon was shown in.

"Good evening, sir," he said, in a grave, important tone.

Standish fancied there was a triumphant gleam in his light grey eyes.

"Good evening, Dillon. I am looking forward with curiosity to your communication. Sit down."

"Hope you'll be satisfied, sir!" said Dillon, drawing a chair and taking out a small note-book, which he laid before him on the table. "I have done my best, but it has been a difficult job, and I did not feel at liberty to speak until I had my chain of evidence complete. If you'll allow me, I'll begin at the beginning." He uttered a loud "hem!" and looking at the

book before him for a moment, proceeded :
" When you applied to me last September
—the 20th, I see," Standish nodded—" and
I went down to Fordsea, I found the usual
sentimental difficulties. I could get over
these, you see, if I were a regular police
detective, but as it was, I was in your
service, and must not go to view the poor
lady till everything was interfered with.
But I persuaded the old Nurse (who had
more brains than the rest) to let me have
a *very* private view. I saw how the body
lay, the head a good deal bent forward as
if slipping off the pillow, the face so calm
and peaceful that she could have had no
glimpse of whoever was going to deal her
her death blow. I took a good look round ;
but I could not stay long, because Mrs.
McHugh was horridly afraid the Colonel
would find her out, and he had given strict
orders that no one but the women who

attended to her should be let in after the jury had viewed the body."

He paused, but Standish sat silently gazing at him.

"I got a good deal of information talking to the servants till I knew the life of the family, which seemed peaceful and happy enough," he resumed, "and at the funeral I had a long look at Mr. Egerton. He struck me very particularly. He's as handsome a man as you'd see in a day's march. But there was a devil of some kind in his eyes, and if ever a man was in mortal agony of grief, *he* was. The husband was quiet and resigned compared to him. Mr. Egerton looked to my mind like a man conscience-stricken. Of course, I had heard a goodish bit about him—how he was wanting to marry the young lady, Mrs. Callander's sister, and all that. But it seemed odd to me that he never came

near her, nor Miss Oakeley. Then you
gave me full right to examine the room, to
put the ladder across the window, and to
talk to Miss Wynn. You remember, she
thought she had heard the bar of the
window fall. Well, sir, I saw clear enough
that she thought there was more in it than
a mere vulgar murder with robbery, and
that she was particularly anxious *not* to
give me a clue; in short, that there was
something in it she didn't want me to find
out, and I began to smell a rat. I began
to think ' has the handsome fine gentleman,
that has been like a brother in a manner
of speaking, anything to do with it?'
Jealousy has been at the bottom of such a
pile of crime."

Standish moved uneasily, and uttered a
half-articulate exclamation. "You were
saying——?" suggested Dillon.

"Nothing! Did you then discard

the theory of the sailor's guilt in the matter?"

"Yes, sir; pretty soon. I'm coming to that. Then, sir, I thought of *you*. You are a good-looking chap, and easy in manners, a'most like a *Amurikan*, and the widower's reluctance to see you was rather remarkable; but I didn't hold to that very long. I never could get to speak to the young lady often enough. *She* knew a thing or two, but she was as close as wax. I gave up the idea of the Spanish sailors for a good many reasons. First, how the deuce could these men know that Colonel Callander was not sleeping in his wife's room? They couldn't gossip with the servants, for they didn't speak their lingo; next, how could they know where the ladder was kept? Of course, they might have overhauled the premises some other night, but it's not likely, Then, I defy any stranger to have lifted up that bar and stepped in right against that dressing-table without making noise enough to disturb a timid woman, unless *she knew who was making it,* and that is not a pleasant nor a probable idea."

" My God, no ! " cried Standish.

" Now, you see, from the way the poor thing was lying, her face was to the window, a stranger coming in by it and pushing the dressing-table must have roused her. She would have seen him, screamed, and, even if killed, her face, her position, would have been totally different."

" To what conclusion does this lead you ? " asked Standish eagerly.

" That the murderer entered by the door of her room ; that his step, his presence, was so familiar that he could approach almost to touching her without creating disturbance or alarm, and then as she lay, still and unresisting, he struck her dead with one blow in the vital spot left undefended by her position."

Standish was a man of great nerve and self-control, but he changed colour at the horrible and degrading suspicion so ruth-lessly presented to him by the unmoved detective.

" No, sir," he resumed, " no stranger struck that blow ! In addition to these conclusions, which any man of common-sense might have arrived at, I observed, on the outside of her door, a little splash, a mere spark, of blood, low down near the floor, and a speck near the handle, which those dunderheads, the police, had not detected. You see, they were all so taken up with the notion that the murderer came in from outside, that they never looked beyond the interior of the room itself, except to search the poor servants' boxes, I believe! Besides these, I picked up, half under the bed, where, no doubt, it had been pushed by some of the feet that trod there, this bit of a silver ornament." He drew it from an inner pocket, and laid it before Standish, who stared at it with distressed eyes.

"You don't happen to have seen it before, Mr. Standish?"

"No, certainly not," replied Standish sharply, while he thought with dismay of Dorothy's description of the broken silver shell with the half-holes at one side.

"Well, sir, I thought you *might* have seen it. I showed it once to Miss Wynn, and *she* said she had never seen it before, though her eyes didn't back her up! That little bit of silver has given me a heap of trouble. I have hunted to and fro to find the other bit of it, but I did at last."

"For God's sake get on!" cried Standish.

" What have you discovered?　Who *do*
you suspect?"

" Hear me out," replied Dillon, sitting
upright, and assuming a more earnest look.
" I made up my mind when I rubbed away
those sparks of blood, that someone *in* the
house did the deed, someone to whom the
poor lady was accustomed, whose presence
did not disturb her, or frighten her, who
could come in and out, and knew the ways
of the place, where the ladder was kept,
and how long it would be before anyone
would come to find her stiff and stark!
Those strange sailors would *never* have
dared to come into a house with a master
and two men sleeping in it!　No, sir; the
hand that struck the blow was her
husband's!"

" You are raving!" exclaimed Standish.

" No, I am not, sir.　Listen!　From
many a trifling indication I got out of

Collins, and the old nurse, I believe the unfortunate man was eaten up with jealousy. The more I watched him—and I have shadowed him for months—the more convinced I grew, that, in some mad fit, he put an end to her, and then tried to mislead us all by laying that ladder on to the window-ledge !"

"It is impossible!" ejaculated Standish.

"No, it a n't! Jealousy is the under-miningest thing out. It works like rats through a wall, gnawing and gnawing for many a long day unheard, till all at once its ugly head gets out to the light to kill and to destroy! Ah, Mr. Standish, the biggest lot of cruel deeds I have traced home took me straight to jealousy!"

Standish stared at him with blank, bewildered eyes.

"Well, though I was pretty sure it was he as did the deed, it was very hard to get

proof. I followed him pretty close ; where-
ever he went I was by him in some disguise
or another, and an awful time he has had
of it. From all I can see, I'd say hanging
is a trifle to what he has gone through!
Still, I could never get a glimpse of any
knife that had ornaments on the sheath
answering to *this*. Another thing puzzled
me—he always kept in with Egerton. I
got to see Egerton more than once, but he
was uncommon haughty and snuff-the-
moon in his ways. I wasn't good enough
to touch with a pair of tongs—Oh, dear no!
I'd have rather proved *him* guilty than the
other poor fellow. Latterly I've begun
to think he suspects the truth. Anyhow,
after waiting and watching, I got what I
wanted at last.

" When Colonel Callander came back
from the Continent the other day, I began
to hang about, and pay a visit now and

again to that respectable, civil - spoken man, Mr. Collins, and one morning I found him packing up the Colonel's duds, so I sat down and discoursed him a bit, watching him sorting the things. Presently he came to pistols, and a queer, long, narrow, foreign - looking knife, with an inlaid handle, and shell - like bits of silver stuck on to the sheath. It was uncommon like the queer sort of weapons hung up in Mr. Egerton's rooms, but the ornaments were different. I took it to the light to examine it, with my back to Mr. Collins, and tried this bit where one of the ornaments was jagged and broken. It fitted perfectly, thoroughly !"

"Still——" urged Standish, starting up, and moving restlessly to the fireplace.

"One moment," said Dillon, raising his hand. "The man who had seen the figure carrying the ladder, I ought to mention, in

13*

conversing with me, said it was a broader, larger man than Egerton, though about his height. Last of all," he continued, speaking more quickly, " I followed the Colonel to Fordsea, where he wandered about on land and sea. He was always going off in a boat with that old tar—you know him !— or else he'd be off, striding so fast that there was no keeping up with him, to the little churchyard by the hill-side, with a basket of flowers for the grave. At last I hired a dog-cart, and used to drive past as if quite on my own business. He never noticed ! Twice I saw him outside groping under some gorse bushes that grew above the low wall. You know the wide view there is all around. Not a soul was to be seen stirring. I drove past, and waited under a piece of broken bank a little further on. I told the boy I had with me to hold the reins, as I wanted to gather some of the ferns about there, and I gradually got my head over the bank, and saw the Colonel coming slowly down the road. I watched till he disappeared on his way back, then I went on picking 'specimens' here and there, till I came pretty nigh where I had watched him stooping down. Not a soul was to be seen. When I was there in the autumn time, there used to be bits of boys herding sheep and goats, but there were none now. When I got about the part where I had noticed the Colonel, I looked well around under the bushes, and at last I came upon a spot where the grass looked a bit disturbed and mixed with mould, as if someone had been digging for roots. I took the bearings of it, and went away back to Fordsea with enough leaves and twigs to set up a botanist. Very early next morning, I found the Colonel was going off to London, so I bought a trowel, and then I watched him start off in the train. As soon as I saw him safe, I trudged away to the place I had marked. I would take no one with me. It was easy to dig, for the soil had been lately stirred, and scarce a foot below the surface I came to a gold chain and locket, then a bracelet, then I picked out three or four rings, then a gold bangle, all messed with mould. There are more there, but these are enough for me."

He took a brown paper parcel from his pocket, and opening it carefully, displayed the trinkets, soiled and bent.

Standish took up and examined each. He was stunned, yet did not let himself go. Dillon was not the man to whom one should make an unguarded admission.

" Your extraordinary ingenuity has unearthed an extraordinary story," he said at length. " The circumstantial evidence against Colonel Callander is of course very strong, but it is not conclusive."

" Perhaps not," returned Dillon carelessly, " still I think there is enough to justify me in applying to the Eastport magistrates for the reward and detailing my reasons for asking it."

" No doubt," rejoined Standish, coolly, seeing Dillon's drift, while the revolting consequences of publicity rushed into his mind.

The arrest of Colonel Callander, the terrible stain on Mabel's character which his fatal jealousy, however unjustifiable, would leave, and backed by Mrs. Callander's evil tongue it would be indelible—and Dorothy! Whatever it cost, Dorothy must be saved from further shocks, deeper pain even than any she had gone through.

" I do not suppose Colonel Callander's family would wish to rob you of a reward

which you have so justly earned by your
zeal and perseverance, though certainly I
little anticipated the curious direction your
enquiries have taken! Your own experience must have shown you how misleading
circumstantial evidence very often is,
further search might show a different side
to the story!—suppose I promise you
another thousand if, by your trained skill
and natural acuteness, you discover any
other solution to the mystery?"

"There is no other to be found. Still
there is no reason why the true facts
might not be kept dark, and all notoriety
and scandal, and sensational paragraphs,
avoided. It's worth paying a second
thousand for that alone. Eh? Just think
of it all! The assertions about the
Colonel's discoveries, the contradictions
and counter-assertions. Why it would
be months and months before that nice

young lady would be able to take up a paper."

"Very probably," returned Standish still calmly. "It is natural to dread such publicity; still, it may be more just to Colonel Callander to pursue your researches and see if some key cannot be found to the extraordinary riddle your discoveries present."

"Look here, Mr. Standish," said the detective impatiently, "you are a little too exacting. Why should I work any harder for that second thousand than I have done? The more we seek, the worse the case will be against your friend. The best piece of service you can do him and all the family is to keep it all dark. I don't believe the poor fellow is quite right in the upper storey. Take a day to think over it— and if you won't seal my lips with a second thousand, why I'll make sure of the first through the magistrates of East-port."

" You are——" began Standish quickly, then paused half a second, and added : " a remarkably shrewd fellow !"

" Ay! that is better," returned Dillon with an unpleasant laugh. " Anyhow, I suppose you have seen these things before?" pointing to the jewels.

" Some of them, certainly," replied Standish.

" I thought so." He began to roll them up carefully. " I need not trespass any longer. I'll call to-morrow about this time for your answer. I'm pretty sure what it will be. I think you are only wasting time."

He put his book and the packet of jewels in his breast pocket, and with a keen lingering look into the eyes of his companion, said abruptly :

" Good evening to you, Mr. Standish."

Paul had rarely felt so stunned and helpless as when the door closed on Dillon, and the strong grasp he had kept upon himself relaxing, he let his thoughts dwell freely on the extraordinary summary which the detective had just laid before him. What a hideous climax to the dismal tragedy of poor Mabel's death! And Callander, that kindly, upright, chivalrous fellow, what a mental wreck he must have become, how maddened by disease and his mother's insinuations, before he could have laid a destroying hand on his adored wife!

Paul's heart thrilled with painful pity, when he thought of what the man's terrible sufferings must have been! But was Dillon right in his conclusion? Was there not a loophole of escape somewhere from the ghastly conviction that Callander was the murderer? and that he should have suspected him—Paul—of having been so base as to tamper with his own ward's fidelity to her husband !

"Thank God! Dorothy had the pluck to clear me from so vile an imputation," he thought. " I wish Callander would fulfil his promise of writing to me! No! I will not believe it yet, in spite of that man's wonderful chain of evidence. Yet it is amazingly complete, and somehow Callander's extraordinary indifference as to the capture of the assassin had always struck me as unnatural ! What is best to be done ? If a whisper gets out of the true story (if it is true)—the scandal-mongers and gossips won't leave that poor girl a shred of character ! The worst of it is, there is just enough folly and weakness at the bottom of this disastrous story, to make it a little difficult to deal with frankly—I am afraid we must silence Dillon. I will only do so under colour of extended search for information. I will never admit that I believe his inferences, his admission! It was to the brute's devilish interest to prove poor Callander guilty!—and Dorothy! What shall I do as regards Dorothy—how shall I ever break the terrible fact that her brother-in-law, the man she loved and respected so heartily, was Mabel's murderer? Need she ever know it? I am afraid in justice to that scoundrel Egerton I must tell her, some day, but not yet! This frightful trial has told upon her! There's a brave heart, and a clear brain, sheathed in her slight delicate frame. Poor little Dorothy, how tender she is in spite of the flashes of fiery spirit that light up her eyes—such a loving nature. Her frank affection to me is touching. I wish I were older for her sake, I might be of more use to her, but as that cannot be, I wonder if

I married Henrietta Oakeley whether we might make a happy home for her? They are very fond of each other, and Henrietta is rather handsome, a good match in many ways. How can I branch off to merely selfish considerations with this dreadful history fresh before me? What egotists we are—I am! I will run down to Fordsea if I possibly can to-morrow, and see Callander. Meantime, is it too late to see Dorothy and Henrietta to-night? Yes, it is past ten. I'll catch them at breakfast to-morrow morning and say I am going to join Callander and get him to come back with me, that will keep them quiet, and after—well, God knows. It is impossible to form any plan. Heaven grant me some good inspiration! everything looks woefully dark.

*   *   *   *   *

Dorothy had not yet come downstairs

when Standish presented himself at Miss Oakeley's breakfast-table next morning.

"Why, Paul—I mean, Mr. Standish—what in the world brings you here at this unearthly hour?" cried Henrietta, who was standing on the hearth-rug before a bright coal and wood fire, teaching a beautiful fluffy Yorkshire terrier high principle, in the guise of resisting sugar when offered for a "Gladstone dog."

"I ought to make a thousand apologies," returned Standish. "I am going down to Fordsea, just to see what Callander is about, and, as I cannot get away till the afternoon, I thought I would venture to look in on you first."

"I am delighted to see you, and very pleased you are going to look for that poor man. Do try and induce him to come abroad and to keep with us. The way he wanders about is quite alarming. Dorothy has not made her appearance yet. She is generally late, poor thing! She is always so mournful. It is really rather trying. I think she would feel more comfortable if we could find the wretched murderer and hang him!"

"Hush!" said Standish, quick and low. "Here she is!" Henrietta's heedless words sent a cold thrill of pain through him.

When Dorothy found herself face to face with Standish, her large serious eyes lit up, and a welcoming smile gladdened her sad mouth. "How early you are, Paul! Has anything happened?" the smile dying away. "You look as if you had not slept all night—so ill and worn!" gazing anxiously in his face.

"I am all right, Dorothy; only, as I have been explaining to Miss Oakeley, I intend to run down to Fordsea, if I can manage it, this afternoon, and I wanted to see you first."

" You are going to find Herbert ? Oh, thank you, dear Paul."

" Do sit down and have some breakfast, both of you. Collins, lift the covers,' cried Miss Oakeley.

"It is curious, your coming this morning," said Dorothy, unfolding her table napkin. " I think some fairy must have whispered that I had a letter for you."

" For me ? Who from ?" asked Standish, surprised.

"Oh, I did not read it, but it was enclosed in one from Miss Boothby, who said she did not know your address.

" From Miss Boothby ? " exclaimed Standish. "This is most astonishing." He opened it, and had a little difficulty in keeping his face quite steady and unchanged when he read:

"Dear Sir,

"I am directed by Mrs. Callander to beg you will not hesitate to draw upon her, even to a large amount, should you require funds for the use of Colonel Callander, in connection with the late distressing event. — I am, Sir, Yours faithfully,

"C. Boothby."

"The unhappy old woman knows the truth," was Paul's mental comment.

"What does she say? Don't be mysterious, Mr. Standish," cried Henrietta Oakeley.

Dorothy did not speak, but she fixed such questioning, tender, sympathising eyes on her guardian, that he longed to open his heart to her.

"There is very little in it. There, read it, Dorothy." She took it from his hand, and read it aloud.

"Well, really my aunt is more of a trump than I believed," said Henrietta exultantly.

"There is something rather strange about this letter," said Dorothy thoughtfully.

"Let us believe, with Miss Oakeley, that her aunt is a trump," he returned, and applied himself to his breakfast.

44*

CHAPTER VI.

"COLONEL CALLANDER'S LETTER."

WITH all his diligence Standish found, when he reached his rooms that afternoon, he had so little time left that it would be almost an impossibility to catch the five-thirty train to Eastport. He was, however, ready to make the attempt, when, among the notes and letters which had come since he started in the morning, an unusually thick envelope, directed in Callander's handwriting.

This changed his plans. It would be foolish to start before reading what Callander had to say, and doing so would compel him to lose the train.

He opened the letter, glanced at it, and ringing for the man who waited on him, hastily directed that no visitor should be admitted. Then, drawing his chair near the window, he began, with interest which deepened at every word, to read the long epistle addressed to him.

"I have been going to write to you, Standish, ever since Dorothy proved to me how greatly I have wronged you in my mind. I have begun once or twice, but, somehow, my brain would not keep clear or steady. There is such a cloud troubling and confusing me; but last night, as I lay awake, battling with my thoughts as usual, something seemed to break away in heart or head, and light came to me.

"I don't think I am mad, but I am not what I used to be, and there is a strange spirit—not my own—urging me at times, with a force I cannot resist, to do many things. Ever since Dorothy showed me the truth, I have wanted to tell you every-thing, for you loved *her*, not as I thought, but as a true elder brother, and you will understand me—perhaps you will help me.

" When she left me in India it was a rueful day. Then I was ill ; after, I re-covered. Her letters were not the same ; they were cold, constrained. How mad I grew, with an agonised longing to see her again, to hold her in my arms ! My mother wrote often. She did not like you ; I do not know why, but she did not. She was always repeating how my darling and Dorothy preferred being with you to any-one else, even to Egerton, who was so superior. It was a long time before she roused the devil within me, but she did at last. Then I came home. The voyage was a long warfare between the heaven of anticipated reunion, and the hell of doubt.

I used to be so secure of her, of myself, of everything. Now, sleeping or waking, I was always struggling on the verge of precipices over which it was destruction to fall.

"When she met me in London, she was so sweet and kind that I thought all was well, that she was the same beloved Mabel I had left, that I was all to her I had been. Whether my joy at meeting was too fierce, too intense, I cannot tell; but in a few—a very few—days, I thought I felt a change; a faint, gentle chill, like the first breath of the night-wind; but I put the idea from me. I fought with it for days and weeks; sometimes I had gleams of happiness and security too delicious for earth. Then my mother would suggest hellish doubts; I do not suppose she thought I would brood over them as I did, but——God forgive her! All this time I saw that Egerton was seeking Dorothy for his wife. So far as anything could interest or please me, I was pleased. At last I proposed to Mabel, who seemed to me unwell and ill at ease, that we should take a journey together somewhere, away from Dorothy, from the children, from everyone. I made her acceptance or rejection of this scheme the test of her feeling for me. I quivered with terror as I suggested it. Well, she accepted. During that drive to Rookstone, which was the last gleam of Heaven on my path, and for a while I had a little peace—not for long— she grew pale, and cold, and nervous. I went to London ; there she wrote to me in a curious, constrained tone. She said she was not strong enough to bear such a journey as I proposed! That decided me to kill her and you. I thought it, mind, not with fury, but with a calm, judicial sense of executing a judgment. The only mode by which I could keep myself in hand was by preserving silence. Wife, children, friends, fair fortune, every good, had become cruellest evil, torturing me with poisoned darts. I used to sit silent and deadly still in your midst, holding back the madman's rage to kill—as best I might!

" At last, one evening, just before you left us, I came into the drawing-room, and found Dorothy putting flowers in a basket. The tea-table was set. I asked her where Mabel was. She said, ' out driving with your mother.' ' And where is Standish ? ' ' He will be here, soon, Mabel expects him.' I stood with my arm on the mantel-piece, gazing into the glass, yet seeing nothing, and thinking—thinking. Suddenly I saw the reflection of Mabel, coming through the open window. She must have come from the dining-room into the verandah, and so

in by the window nearest me. She did
not seem to see there was anyone in the
room, but went to the round table, which
was always covered with books—you know
the oval mirror that leant forward over it?
Well, in that I saw her slip a folded paper
into a book—the lowermost of a small pile
—a green one with gold edges lay on the
top. I kept my eyes on it, but as her back
was to me, I sat down noiselessly in a
chair. Presently she turned and perceived
me. Then she uttered a little cry, came
across the room to me, and kissed me more
tenderly than she had done for many a
day. Then I knew I could kill her! I
pressed my finger and thumb round her
soft, white throat—she little knew how
near death was to her for a moment! She
said, 'you hurt me, dear,' smiling in my
face. I let her go, though I thought my
heart would burst. Soon you came in,

and Egerton, and Henrietta; while you spoke together, I went to the table, and took away the book. *She* was at the tea-table, and never noticed. I hid the book, and afterwards found in it a folded sheet of paper, on which, in *her* writing were these words: 'I cannot resist your influence; it was always too strong! For God's sake do not urge me to leave all for you—you ought to have mercy on such weakness! I fear *him* more every day—for he suspects, I know he does—and that idea overwhelms me. Go! keep far away! Whatever happens, my heart will break! I do beseech you to go!' There was neither address nor signature; but the expression 'your influence, it was always too strong,' pointed to *you*—it seemed confirmation strong as holy writ. I have destroyed the paper lest blame should ever touch her."

Here the unfortunate man had evidently

stopped, and resumed after a pause of some hours, perhaps days.

"It is a long, weary tale ; it seems to me that I am writing of another, and I pity him profoundly, as I should never pity myself. My hatred of you grew deep and cunning; there was no base, cowardly act I would not have done, could I have tortured you without bringing disgrace on my own name. But all through my curious, agonising mental struggles, I remembered that my name belonged to my children! You went away the day after, or the day but one.

"That seemed in obedience to her request. My mother said it was an immense relief to her mind that you were safe out of the way. I silenced her fiercely; but even above my burning desire for revenge on you, was my resolution to save my darling from her cruel

comments, her bitter judgment. Brooding
over this, haunted by a hideous vision of
being compelled for my honour's sake to
put away my wife, to drag her through the
mire and filth of legal proceedings, of the
opprobrium of society, of moral annihila-
tion; something whispered to me, 'have
the courage to save her from all this—let
the icy hand of death send her unsullied to
a better world, where the All-seeing alone
can judge her.' The idea would not, did
not, leave me! It had an extraordinary
fascination for me; even now, though I
know my suspicions were wrong, I believe
I did my best for her under the circumstances.

"It was not murder, no—it was the act
of tenderest love. I wanted no revenge on
her—I only wanted to save her from shame
and bitterest grief. As a Christian, I believe in the happiness of the hereafter, and

her sin was but slight, *now*, only a womanish weakness which laid her at the mercy of a stronger will—a will backed by the force of her habitual obedience to it. If I hesitated, she might—almost surely would—break the social laws we are bound to uphold, and become an outcast. Had she not in her veins the blood of a mother who had outraged them? So I resolved to send my beautiful Mabel to Heaven, even while *I* affronted Hell for her sake. My logic is sound, Standish, is it not? She would have gone hence blameless! From *me* an inexorable judge would have demanded the price of her blood, and for her sake I am content to pay it!"

Here came some disconnected passionate sentences about the freedom of choice, the happiness of Heaven, the injustice of fate, the boundless love of God, the possibility

of the Persian belief in the final purifica-
tion of the guiltiest by fire proving to be
true, and Callander resumed his narrative
more calmly.

" This idea fascinated me.   I had, from
the fear of doing my dearest one harm in
some ungovernable fit of despair, remained
in my own room on the plea of indifferent
health, and there I thought out my plan.
One night, just after you had gone, I had
put on my smoking jacket, and sat down
to think, but I could not smoke, my mind
was a sort of fiery mist, all the past un-
rolled itself, the happy hours, the sweet-
ness and purity of my darling: should I
allow shame to touch her ? A voice said to
me, ' the hour has come, let it not pass.'   I
rose up, and took a long keen knife, which
Egerton had given me as a curiosity.   It
was fine and sharp.   I went softly but
boldly to her room.   I did not fear to meet

anyone; I was not overstepping my right.
Her door opened without noise; she was
not asleep; she said drowsily, 'Is it you,
Herbert?'

" 'Yes,' I said, 'I cannot sleep. I think
the sleeping medicine is here.'

" 'It is, perhaps, on the mantel-piece.' I
went to look, and stood there long, listening, till her calm regular breathing told
me she slept, then I took the candle
and stole behind her. Her head had
fallen forward, her pretty hair was
gathered into a thick knot, and I saw
the place where old Dowden, our surgeon
once told us (myself and one or two of
'ours') where a thrust might cause in-
stantaneous death; with a silent prayer
that I might not fail, or cause her a
moment's pain, I struck deep and true
with a steady hand. There was a slight
sigh; the fair head fell a little further for-

ward, and she was free—quite free; now she knows my motives, she forgives me! I turned to go round, and looked into her angel face, when I trod on the sheath which had fallen on the carpet, and knocked against the bed. This shocked me more than I can tell you, for there something terribly, sublimely sacred in that silent, motionless figure; to stir it rudely seemed sacrilege. I know not why, but I could *not* stay after that. J. wiped the knife in my handkerchief. There was very little blood upon it; I wiped what I could from the roots of her beautiful golden hair. Then I left her lying there. I was not quite so steady when I closed the door behind me, as when I opened it; for when I reached my room, I found I had dropped the handkerchief. I went back and found it against the door.

"I felt a sort of relief as I sat down and

thought of what I had done. She was safe. I had taken her sweet life, but I had kept her from evil tongues, from a terrible fate, and embalmed her in the loving memory of those who could never reproach her. But now came the reflection that were I suspected the truth would ooze out, and the judgment upon her would be more unmerciful than ever. I had acted on impulse. Now it was my bounden duty to conceal my crime (as it would have been called), for her sake first, for my children's, for the completion of my revenge on you. There was no time to lose. I lit the fire, which was always laid ready in my room, and thrust in the handkerchief, that it might leave no trace. I hung up the knife in its accustomed place. I went softly to the side door. I often wandered out of a night unknown to anybody, and the hinges were well oiled, then I took the ladder from the shed, and placed it as it was found. I crossed it, and lifted the bar which secured the shutters inside, letting it fall with what seemed to me a terrible noise, and entered the room again. By the dim night-light I kissed my darling, and put back the dressing-table which I had slightly moved. Then I gathered up the watch, the locket, rings, bracelets that lay on the table, and stole away once more to my own room. I rolled up the jewels in three parcels, and locked them away. Then I put on my dressing-gown, and sat down as if to write—so I waited, waited for the discovery. I think I must have become insensible or slept. I felt awfully exhausted. At last Collins came with my tea. I drank it, and still sat wondering what would happen next. Then Mrs. McHugh

15*

burst in——You know the rest. I seemed
but half alive after, and it was amazing
how things lent themselves to my rude
plan of concealment.

" Now, I have nearly told you everything,
Standish. My brain is growing dull and
dreamy. I have always wondered why
Egerton shrank from me. Dorothy has
explained why. She has restored my
faith in you. When I knew the truth, it
made me pitiless. The irreparable evil
wrought by my mother infuriated me.
I rushed to her and told her that, thanks
to her cruel tongue, her son was what she
would call a murderer. I wonder it did
not kill her! My sufferings have been
great, though I have had long spells of
torpidity. Since I came down to Fordsea,
I have been conscious of an awful irresistible weariness of life. Like the unhappy Moor, whose story is so like my

own, 'My occupation's oe'r '—no, not yet! I must settle my account with Egerton. I cannot rest till that is finished; does he know this, that he keeps out of the way? Well, I can find him. If he lives as I do, I would not seek to cut short his career. I went a few days ago to her grave; I go often, but this time I accomplished what I long desired. I dug up the jewels I had buried on the hill-side, to get that bangle she always wore; I have longed for it. I seem to see her white arm and the glittering gold ring upon its snow. Do not touch the rest, Standish, let them lie where I laid them. Take care of my poor children, you and Dorothy must take care of them. I am so desperately tired. When shall I find rest? Your friend, as of old,

" HERBERT CALLANDER."

Standish was very white, and his teeth were set, when he laid down the last sheet of this long, sad, startling letter.

It was too true, then, Dillon's clever disentangling of the puzzle! What a terrible tragedy this destruction of two lives! His generous heart ached for the ruin, the injustice, wrought by a spiteful tongue, by the selfish recklessness of a man too absorbed in a guilty passion to hesitate at the sacrifice of friendship, honour, loyalty, or even the happiness of the woman he professed to love.

It was brutal, insensate, but Standish had no time to think of Egerton now. Callander's case was a serious one. He must not be suspected; the terrible truth must not leak out. For the unfortunate criminal himself, Standish felt the most profound pity. He could not look on him as responsible. Disease was gaining fast upon him, but a jury would probably take a very different view of his condition. Come what might, he must be shielded from the consequences of his desperate deed. It must be kept profoundly secret. Dillon must be silenced. No breath of the dreadful truth must reach Dorothy's ears; it was enough to kill her with horror. He (Standish) must get him out of the country. But how? Could he send the unhappy half, if not not wholly, insane man to wander alone, and put the climax to the dreadful story by murdering Egerton, or himself, or both, and so display the disgraceful facts to the world, covering the memory of poor, timid Mabel with obloquy?

Nor, if Callander went, as Henrietta Oakeley proposed, with her and Dorothy to make a temporary home abroad, would he ever know a moment's peace! The fatal brain disease from which he believed Callander was suffering was certain to increase, and God only knew what delusion might urge him to attack Dorothy. Standish shuddered and started to his feet as the idea flashed across him. For some moments he was stunned and incapable of forming any plan. But by an effort, a strong exertion of self-control, he pulled himself together. He would go to Eastport that night. There was one more train. He could, at least, go and speak with Callander, and see how far he was capable of hearing reason. He had been such a fine, high-minded, unselfish, chivalrous fellow; surely some sparks of the old light must linger in his poor, distraught brain. He might feel the necessity for a friend's sheltering guidance. How could he, even in the profoundest aberration, lay a destroying hand upon his sweet, gentle wife? Had he been himself, and fit to guide her, a few wise, loving words would have put all right between them, and freed her from the unholy mesh in which Egerton had entangled her. But looking at the past by the light of the present, Standish felt convinced of what he formerly dimly guessed at; that for some reason Mabel had of late grown to fear her husband.

"I waste time pondering here when I ought to act," he exclaimed, and taking Callander's long confession, he enclosed it in a fresh, strong envelope, sealed it, and writing on it his own name, he added, "to be destroyed in case of my death."

Then, with a heavy heart, he put a change of raiment into his bag, and having snatched a hasty meal, drove to Waterloo Station. He was rather too soon for the eight-thirty train to Eastport, so he sat in the corner of the waiting-room, his legs stretched out, his hands deep in his pockets, and his travelling cap over his eyes.

There were few people about, and Standish, wrapped in his own troubled thoughts, was not conscious of their presence. He was, therefore, startled when a tall, well-dressed man suddenly accosted him.

"Halloa, Standish! Where are you bound for?"

"Ah, St. John! I—I didn't know you were in town."

"I have been up for ten days!" returned St. John, "and I am going down to Aldershot to see my sister, Lady Dashwood. Her husband is quartered down there. I'm due at headquarters the day after to morrow. I was dining with your handsome cousin, Miss Oakeley, and missed my train. Little Miss Wynn, Mrs. Blackett, her son, and old Colonel Conway, made up the party. They said you had gone down to Fordsea to look after poor Callander."

"Missed my train too," returned Standish abruptly.

"Both in the same predicament, eh? Your ward, Miss Wynn, is looking as if she had cried her eyes out. 'Pon my soul! it's too bad to see such a pretty creature fretting herself to fiddle-strings."

"Can't wonder at it!" growled Standish. "When you think of the awful blow she has had. I am glad she appeared; she is inclined to shut herself up."

"That's foolish—ain't it?"

"It's one of those things that can't be reasoned about."

"Have you seen Egerton?" pursued St. John.

"Egerton? No; he is not in England.

"Oh, yes he is! I saw him in a hansom just now, coming across the Bridge."

"Are you sure?"

"As sure as I am that I see *you!*"

"I did not know he was coming back so soon!" exclaimed Standish, and fell into deep thought. It would be hard to meet Egerton and refrain from shooting him; he was such an utter scoundrel. Yet he must keep him from encountering Callander. If this happened, some frightful scene would ensue which would expose the whole truth to public gaze. His unexpected return would complicate matters considerably.

"So I suppose they will marry now, and then he'll dry her tears for her," St. John was saying when Standish again listened.

"Who—what?" he asked, rather impatiently.

"Why your ward's. I suppose when the mourning is over he'll marry her—Egerton will, eh? They are engaged?"

"No, they are not. They never were. She never wanted him."

"Do you mean to say she would refuse such an offer? Why, there must be some other fellow in the field. Yourself, eh? Always heard you were a fascinating sort of chap. But the little girl has no tin, I fancy."

"Good - night!" exclaimed Standish, starting up, "I must get my ticket," and he rushed off abruptly.

"What a blatant idiot that St. John is," thought Standish, as he settled himself in a corner of his compartment; "and it's uncommonly lucky that Dorothy had the discrimination to see through Egerton's spurious love-making! Nine girls out of every ten would have been carried away

by it! What preserved my little Dorothy?
Profound penetration? No, that's too big
a thing. True instinct?—more likely.
Love for another?—most likely of all; but
who? She is an uncommon little puss—
and—I'm not sure I should quite enjoy
seeing her fondly in love, and going to be·
married! Yet it would be best for her.
This dreadful business will affect her future
—affect it rather disastrously if any trial
and 'esclandre' takes place. If Henrietta
marries, what is to become of Dorothy?—
even if she does not—they have only
drifted together temporarily! What a
womanly little creature Dorothy always
has been! Why, I don't think she has
given me a kiss since she was twelve years
old! Well, she must be taken care of,
whatever happens!" Then, half ashamed of
dwelling so long on Dorothy's possible love
affairs when such grave and tragic matters

lay before him, Standish turned his thoughts to the problem of Callander's future.

Though feeling that the unfortunate man was scarcely responsible, he was conscious of a distinct repugnance to the idea of meeting, and probably touching hands with the murderer of his gentle, loveable ward.

"The mind must have been hopelessly impaired," mused Standish, "before a man like Callander, a chivalrous gentleman, would deliberately strike a woman in her sleep, and that woman his own beautiful wife! What may he not attempt in the future? Yet without displaying the very seamy side of the story, how can I appeal for legal authority to put him under restraint? It's all infernally puzzling. Much will depend on the condition in which I find him. I almost hope he may never quite regain his original mental condition,

or remorse for the fatal crime he has committed will be more than he could bear.
As to letting Dorothy live with him—that
is not to be thought of."

*   *   *   *   *

It was past eleven when Standish reached
the well-known Pier Hotel at Fordsea.

Colonel Callander, the waiter said, had
gone to his room some time before. So
Standish would not hear of disturbing
him.

"I can see him to-morrow morning," he
said. "At what hour does Colonel Callander breakfast?"

"Nine sharp, sir. He goes out to boat
or bathe very early, and comes in about
eight-thirty—to-night he ordered fish and ,,
kidneys for breakfast, as he seemed to
expect you might come, sir."

"Oh, very well!—give me some brandy
and soda, and I will go to bed too."

This apparent hope of seeing himself, seemed a good sign to Standish. If Callander was only capable of taking a rational view of his own position, it would simplify matters; but Standish dreaded the final stages of that most terrible disease—softening of the brain—which reduces the most gifted to the level of the " beasts that perish."

It was some time before Standish could sleep—when he did, he slept heavily.

The emotions of the day had fatigued as much as physical exertion would have done.

When he woke, the sun was high in the heavens, and sparkling brightly on the rippling waters of the bay. All things seemed smiling with the infantile joyousness which the sea, in its gently playful moods, often expresses.

It struck Standish with indescribable

sadness. He shrank from the approaching interview with profound repugnance, and a depressing sense of not being equal to the task he had undertaken.

When dressed, and ready—it was nearly half-past eight, and taking his hat, he sallied forth—thinking it might be less oppressive to meet Callander first in the open air.

As he strolled slowly towards the hut where Old Jack, the boatman, sheltered himself among his boats, drawn up beside it—every step recalled the happy hours he had spent on the beach with Mabel and Dorothy, the previous autumn; chiefly with Dorothy ! for as he reviewed that happy holiday-time, he remembered how often the *partie carrée* broke into a *tête-à-tête* division—that Egerton rarely left Mabel till Callander arrived, while Dorothy and himself found so much to occupy and interest them, that they rarely missed the others.

And what an ending to such fair, tranquil, seemingly innocent days! To what a tragic conclusion they were blindly drifting!

Standish found old Jack seated in the stern of one of his boats, smoking a very black pipe, and looking out so earnestly towards the east headland, that he did not hear the approaching step.

"Good morning, Jack!"

"Eh? Mr. Standish! mornin', sir— haven't seen you down here this many a day, sir!"

"No, I've been too busy to take a holiday."

"Not much of a holiday for you to come down *here*, sir!" said the rugged old salt with feeling.

"That's true!" There was a pause—

46*

then Standish asked, "Has the Colonel gone out to bathe to-day."

"Yes, sir! He goes a fishing or bathing every morning when he is down—sometimes I go with him; but bless your 'art sir, he never catches nothing! Forgets he's holding the lines most of the time! He ought to be coming in about now," putting a battered glass to his eye, "I see no sign of him yet. When he gets the oars in his hands, he rows sharp enough. You sit down a bit, sir—he'll not be long—he went away tow'st the Head, where the ladies used to like to row, in the mornings —last autumn? Ah, well!—the ways of providence are past our knowledge!"— With a sigh, and a wise shake of the head, Old Jack resumed his pipe.

CHAPTER VII.

"THE SEA GIVES UP ITS DEAD."

STANDISH accepted the old man's invitation, and, lighting a cigar, took his seat beside him. A long spell of silence ensued.

There is no more taciturn creature in the world than your regular old salt. With his weather eye (whatever that may be) perpetually on the look-out for squalls, or the shifting of the wind, and his mind on the alert to meet the treacherous forces of sea and storm, with all that human foresight and resolution can do to circumvent and conquer them, he does not care to weaken his mental powers with idle words, but out of the stores of slowly accumulated wisdom, he lets drop occasionally pearls and diamonds of tersely expressed opinion, the essence of his crystallised experience.

So Standish and his weather-beaten host (for, had he not offered him the hospitality of his stranded boat?) sat silently side by side, their eyes directed watchfully toward the " Head," as the promontory east of the bay was familiarly called, the thoughts of both centred on the same object.

Time went very slowly, and Standish was quite surprised when half-past nine chimed from the clock of the old town church. " I thought it must be ten at least," exclaimed Standish impatiently.

" It's past his usual time," said Jack, putting up his battered glass again. " He went only for a dip," he said. " If it's your will, sir, I'll just pull out to look for him if we see no sign of him in ten minutes.'

"Do," said Standish eagerly, "and I'll come with you. You may have a long pull."

"The tide will be flowing for quarter of an hour longer," said the boatman, "and with the tide he ought to come pretty quick, but *we'll* find it stiff work."

He got over the side of his boat as he spoke and began very deliberately to put a couple of oars in a lighter one.

"It's the finest morning we have had this month," he said slowly. "He may be tempted to swim about a bit. Still, it might be better to go and look for him."

"Much better," said Standish, assisting the old man to push the light boat over the shingle to the water. As they took their places, three-quarters chimed out, a sou-west wind carrying the sound over the waters.

Standish had been accustomed to row in

his Oxford days, and from time to time
since ; and now, unknown to himself, his
unspoken fears found expression in his
energetic strokes, till at last his old mate
exclaimed, " Gently, by your leave, sir. If
you pull so hard you'll pull me round.
There's no use in hurrying. It's getting a
little fresher, and there's a pretty tidy swell
on.   We might miss the chase in the
trough of the waves. Keep her head to
the wind and I'll give him a hail."

Standing up, old Jack Goold shouted
long and loud the name of the boat taken
out by Colonel Callander that morning,
" *Lively Peggy,* ahoy ! "

In vain ; there was not even an echo to
reply.

Then he returned to his oar, saying simply, " Let's make straight for the
head."

So they rowed on and on, and round and

about, but no trace of the *Lively Peggy* nor her oarsman was to be seen.

Never did Standish lose the profound impression of that weary row, the sickening fear which grew upon him, the hopelessness and sinking of the heart.

At last Jack Goold said, sullenly and hoarsely, " We'd best get back, sir. I don't see how we can do any good. We'd best speak this tug I see coming along on our tack. If you promise something of a reward, they'll keep a look-out. There's no knowing where the boat's drifted."

" The boat, man!" cried Standish, in much agitation. " You don't mean to say you do not think Colonel Callander is in her ? "

" I don't mean nothing, Mr Standish; only it looks baddish seeing no sign of her."

The old man presently hailed the tug,

which ran down to them. Standish
clambered on board, but the old boatman
thought it better to return to his station,
in case they had, by any accident, missed
the object of their search, hoping to find
his boat and its occupant, alike beached
and safe.

It would take much time and space to
describe the growing fears with which
Standish paced the tug's dirty deck, or
stood eagerly scanning the face of the
waters, as they steamed slowly to and
fro.

At length the skipper remarked that if
they stayed thereabouts till night, they
would find nothing; adding, not without
feeling, that he would not give much for the
gentleman's chance if some craft had not
picked him up before this.

Standish agreed with him, and the master
bringing his vessel to as near the Head as

he could safely go, sent his passenger ashore in one of the tug's boats.

The spot he landed on was a small rocky projection not far from a stretch of fine sand which filled a slight indentation of the shore, where Standish had often found Dorothy, with Nurse and the children, hunting for shells and seaweed. A long walk, however, was before him, and his mind was too profoundly disturbed to allow of tender memories. He pressed on at a good pace, thinking hard what was best to be done if Callander had disappeared, or if he returned alive. Both contingencies had its difficulties.

It was a long, painful progress. Nearing the common, he diverged from his direct road to pass Jack Goold's hut. The old man was on the look-out, and, perceiving his approach, came rapidly to meet him.

" What news ? " shouted Standish before they were within speaking distance.

Jack shook his head, and as soon as they stood face to face, said, in a low voice, " Bad — couldn't be worse. A chap has just come down to tell me that my boat has been picked up by the fishing smack *Mary Jane*, with the Colonel's clothes, his watch and chain and purse. The poor gentleman is lost, that's plain enough. Likely got cramp and went down, for he was a strong swimmer."

Standish stood still and silent. Was this the end of the story—the last act of a pitiful tragedy to which two innocent sufferers had been driven by blind fate?

" I suppose it is folly to hope ? " he forced himself to say at last.

" Ay ! no good at all, sir. I don't see as there is a spark of hope, nohow ! He was a grand gentleman," continued the old boatman, beginning to fill his pipe with an unsteady hand. "That kind and thoughtful for them as worked with him ; but one you wouldn't care to say ' no ' to. I don't think he was quite right, sir, since them Spanish swabs murdered his poor lady! By Gad, sir," with sudden fire, "I'd like to string 'em up to the yard-arm with my own hand!"

"It is an appalling *finale*," muttered Standish to himself.

"It is so, sir ; but the Lord, He only knows the heart!"

An utterance which showed Standish the drift of the old man's thoughts.

"Where can I find these fishing-people and the boat ?"

Jack Goold immediately offered to guide him, and, tired as he was with five or six hours' mental and physical strain, Standish had no thought but for the task still before him, and proceeded at once to the well-remembered old dock, where the fishing-smack lay.

The clothes, etc., had been already handed over to the police. These Standish had no difficulty in recognizing. He was assured that all attempt to search for the body would be useless. Some of the currents which existed outside the bay might have swept it out to sea, or the tide might cast it up.

As there was no more to be done at present, Standish, though greatly shaken, was obliged to think of his own duties, public and private. His temporary leave was nearly expired, and his chief had shown him so much consideration, that he was anxious not to out-stay it. Then none save himself must break the sad news to Dorothy. How would she bear this last blow?

He, therefore, telegraphed to Colonel Callander's solicitor to come down himself, or send some capable employé to be on the spot, should action of any kind prove necessary, adding that he would wait his arrival.

A reply wire soon reached him to the effect that Mr. Brierly himself would come down by the three-ten train.

Standish was thus enabled to confer with the greatly distressed lawyer (who was also a personal friend of Callander's) before he started for town.

It was nearly nine o'clock when he reached his rooms, and he debated with himself whether he should attempt to see Dorothy that night or not. "No," was his conclusion; "she shall have this night, at least, undisturbed." Indeed, after the tremendous strain of that trying day, he felt quite unequal to meet her.

Before tasting food, he penned a few
lines to Henrietta which he marked private,
saying he would be with her immediately
after breakfast next day, and entreating her
to keep all newspapers from Dorothy, till
after he had seen her. "They will be sure
to have paragraphs with startling headings
about poor Callander! But he may not be
drowned after all! Why should he not be
picked up, as well as the boat?" thought
Standish, as he rang for the man of the
house, who usually waited on him.

"Take this, or send it by some sure messenger to Miss Oakeley. Give it to Collins
the man there, with this note to himself,
which he must read first."

"Very well, sir. My eldest boy is in,
shall I send him? He is a steady lad,
sir."

"Do so. Let him take a cab at
once."

"Very well, sir; and I forgot to say Mr. Egerton called this afternoon. He said as he could not find you at the club, he came on here. He seemed surprised to hear you had gone down to Fordsea, sir."

"Mr. Egerton?" repeated Standish, his brow contracting; there was another task.

"I shall probably meet him to-morrow."

"Any answer to these, sir?" taking the notes.

"No—none."

The man left the room, but returned almost immediately.

"Mr. Egerton is below, sir. Shall I show him up?"

"Yes; show him up," said Standish, sudden vigour and fire replacing his exhaustion at the sound of his name.

He remained standing, and the next moment Egerton entered.

" Very glad to find you at last," he cried, in his usual genial, pleasant voice, as he advanced, with outstretched hand ; " I am longing to know——"

He stopped, silenced and astonished by the aspect of Standish, his stern face, and the sight of his hand closed and resting on the table, quite irresponsive to Egerton's friendly gesture.

" What is the matter, Standish ? "

" I will explain. You must hear me without interruption, for what I am going to say is a sufficient strain on my self-control. I have heard the whole truth which underlay the tragedy in which we have both played a part. I know the brutal villainy of your conduct towards your friend's wife. I know that the suspicions which should have fallen on you were directed to me, and I have it from Callander himself that he, too, had learned the truth, that he was aware of the debt he owed you, and was resolved to pay it in full; therefore, you are unfit to touch the hand of a gentleman, to sit in the room with a decent woman! You took the heart, the will, of a weak, innocent child by falsest stratagem into your iron, pitiless hands, and for the gratification of a base passion, destroyed her soul's life, as certainly as her murderer struck her dead!"

While he spoke, Egerton's large, dark eyes grew larger, fiercer, and fixed themselves unflinchingly on those of Standish.

"Yes!" he returned, in a hard voice. "This is how, I suppose, a moral, blameless man like yourself looks upon me, and this is how I look upon myself: I found one of the sweetest, fairest creatures my eyes ever rested on, whose indefinable charm fascinated my heart, and thrilled my senses as no other woman among the numbers I

47*

have known ever did before.   I found her
tied to a cold, half indifferent man, whose
age, whose dull nature checked and re-
pressed hers.   She feared him, she wanted
the companionship of a younger, a more
sympathetic man!   She was formed for
me, and all that was needed to secure such
happiness as men and women rarely taste
was that she should take courage and burst
her bonds.   It would have been but a nine
days' wonder, soon forgotten, and I could
have given her *every*thing!   But she dared
not!   God never created an angel purer or
more self-denying than Mabel!   Whether
right or wrong, I have but one regret, that
I did not succeed in carrying her away
from the oppression of her home to the
heaven my love could have created—from
the cruel madman who destroyed her
sweet life, to the shelter of my arms.   My
love for her gave me superior rights!   I

shall never repent or regret my share in the past!"

"You too, are insane," exclaimed Standish amazed at his self-deception, and struck by his allusion to Callander. "You must have lost your balance or been born without moral sense!"

"Moral sense? What is moral sense? the cumbrous lacquer with which the needs of society compel us to overlay our nature! There are circumstances which excuse our casting off this outer husk. But I understand what preachers such as you will think. To the moral sense of your ward Dorothy her sister owes her death. Had she not interfered Mabel would now be living, recovered from the shock of following the dictates of her own heart, and glowing with the joy she gave and received."

"And Callander?" asked Standish sternly.

" Dead, or in a lunatic asylum—what is that to me ? "

" Your recklessness is revolting."

"Is it ? Remember, I have conquered myself for *her* sake! Feeling convinced from some strange innate conviction that Callander murdered his wife, I forced myself to endure his company rather than give cruel tongues any chance of touching the truth. I bore the bitter reproaches of her sister. I *will* bear in silence—no breath from me shall ever tarnish the pure name of my beloved dead! Do you think that all the suffering has been on the husband's and sister's side! You little know the absolute physical agony I have endured! For *her* sake I listen to your abuse without seeking the satisfaction I should otherwise gladly demand! But no! I do not care enough for your opinion—for yourself— or for anything else in life—to enjoy

shooting you! You are of your kind—
honourable, phlegmatic, high principled—
not with living fire in your veins as I have!
We cannot help our natures! But you and
I have the honour of Callander's name, the
safety of his life in our hands, and though
we shall keep far apart in future, we must
guard it well."

" His honour, yes! for the rest—no
earthly judge can touch him now."

" My God ! " cried Egerton with a sudden
revulsion of feeling. " Is he dead ? "

" I have reason to believe so," and
Standish told the occurrences of the day
as rapidly as he could.

" Then that chapter is finished ! " exclaimed Egerton. " *We* can never meet
again as friends; but for the sake of the
dead we must not seem enemies. Dorothy
may rest satisfied with her work," he added
with a sneer.

"She has reason to be satisfied," returned Standish gravely. "Better mourn over her sister's early grave, than blush for a faithless wife, a dishonoured mother."

Egerton stood a moment in silence. Then he said, more to himself than to Standish, "I shall leave England to-morrow." With one steady defiant look into the face of his accuser he left the room and the house. This last interview completed the exhaustion of the day. Standish forced himself to take some food, and then stupefied with fatigue slept heavily till morning. He felt that there was yet a severe trial before him in breaking the news to Dorothy. He profoundly feared the results of such repeated shocks on her sensitive, sympathetic nature. He must guard her from the knowledge that Callander's hand had robbed her of her sister.

*　　　*　　　*　　　*　　　*

When Standish reached Prince's Place next morning he found Dorothy alone at the breakfast table; she was looking a little brighter than usual, and rose to receive him with a welcoming smile.

"I am so glad you have come, dear Paul! I am dying to hear how you and Herbert met. If he is friends with you and trusts to you, he may recover something of his old frame of mind."

"Yes, Dorothy, I will tell you everything," returned Standish, holding her hand half unconsciously in both his own. "But come into the study, we shall be undisturbed! Have you finished your breakfast?"

"Oh! yes, quite—Henrietta has a headache, so she did not come down; but she wants to see you before you go."

While Dorothy spoke she led the way into the study; a small fire was burning, and the window was open upon a neat little garden, where the sunshine of an early spring morning seemed to promise a future crop of grass and flowers.

"It is cold still," said Dorothy, closing the window and turning to Standish, who stood still and silent ; something in his face, in his compassionate eyes, struck her heart.

"Paul—dear Paul—how dreadfully ill you look ! something has happened ! something to Herbert ! Tell me at once ?"

"Yes ! my dearest Dorothy ! We greatly fear—that an accident—bathing—sudden cramp, perhaps——" Standish could hardly form his words.

"Oh Paul ! say it at once. Is he dead ?"

"Sit down, my child," drawing her to the sofa, and holding her hands in his. "We cannot say certainly that he is ! but I fear we shall never see him again—I will tell you all——"

Dorothy listened with wide-open dry eyes.

"Might he not have been taken up by some other ship, Paul?" she exclaimed in a tremulous voice. "Oh! I wanted him to have a few peaceful days with you and me and the poor children, he has been *so* miserable! and you two never met again! It is all too cruel!" She trembled violently but could not weep. "And Mr. Fortescue —you know him—he came with us that day so long ago, in the yacht to Rookstone. Well, he was at luncheon yesterday and said he had seen Herbert at Fordsea, and thought him looking better than he expected; he spoke so nicely, so sympathetically, that I felt cheered. And now all is over—the children are quite orphans! Oh! I feel that he is indeed dead!"

"I rather think he must be! But if he died without much suffering, don't you

think it better for him to be at peace—
perhaps united to Mabel—as Christians are
permitted to believe such things possible ?
Have you no tears, Dorothy ? It frightens
me, dear, to see your poor eyes so dry—to
feel how you tremble."

"I tell you what terrifies me, Paul ! Do
you—do you think he did it himself ?"
and she clung shuddering to him.

"No, certainly not !" returned Standish,
promptly. "Why—he ordered breakfast
for himself and for me (for he seemed to
have expected me), and in his letter he
spoke of objects to live for ! No, Dorothy
—put that thought out of your head."

" He wrote to you, then ?"

"Yes, very kindly and frankly, just like
his old self."

"Ah ! how good he was, how kind he
was—how gentle, how true — why, why
has one bad man been allowed to de-

stroy our happiness ?   My head feels on
fire— —"

" Think of those poor little children, so
unconscious of their desolation," began
Standish, at his wits' end to draw tears
to the poor strained eyes, when the door
burst open and Henrietta, her eyes red
with weeping and a handkerchief in her
hand, came in.

" Oh! Have you told her ? Isn't it too
dreadful? Oh, poor, dear Dorothy, how I
feel for you ! Yet what can your grief be
to mine ? I loved him all my life, quite all
my life," and sitting down, she covered
her face, and sobbed aloud.

" How did you know ? " asked Standish.
" I did not say anything in my note, to
save murdering sleep for one night? "

" It was this morning. Collins read it
it in the papers and told Celestine, and she
ran, of course, to me. I kept out of the

way in my room, for I knew I should talk
to Dorothy, and I told them to keep all
the papers below. Now you must tell me
the whole dreadful story."

Standish complied — noticing the constant fits of trembling that shook Dorothy's
slight frame.

"Now," said Henrietta, rising, "I hope
you will not mind being left alone Dorothy,
but I am going off almost immediately to
catch the mid-day Calais boat. I feel I
ought to break this frightful news to my
aunt. In losing her son she loses everything, and nobody seems to think of her."

"I certainly do!" said Standish, grimly.
"Had it not been for her——" he stopped.

"Oh! yes, I know, she growled and
grumbled and made herself disagreeable,
but then she meant well! At any rate,
Dorothy, I feel I ought to go to Aunt
Callander."

"Yes, Henrietta. I don't mind staying with Nurse, I am so fond of her, and Paul will come and see me. I think I will go and lie down, my head and eyes ache dreadfully."

"Well, do, dear. I shall see you settled before I go."

"Good-bye, Paul. How good and kind you always are to me!" At last the gracious tears came, and Dorothy hurried from the room.

"Thank God she can weep at last!" cried Standish to Henrietta. "For Heaven's sake come back as soon as you can. I feel certain she is going to be ill! But I daresay Mrs. McHugh will take good care of her."

"I declare you don't seem to have a thought for anyone *but* Dorothy," said Henrietta, impatiently.

"Not many," he returned tersely.

Henrietta stared at him.

"You will be sure to telegraph to me to Meurice's if you have any news or in any case. If this day passes over without his return, we have seen the last of poor Herbert!" She again burst into tears, and shaking hands with him, she followed Dorothy upstairs.

Standish returned to his chambers on his way to the Foreign Office, and found a telegram from Brierly :

"Body cast up by tide on western spit. Shall do all that is needful. Come as soon as you can."

Despatching this by a messenger to Miss Oakeley, Standish perforce continued on his way, that he might clear off some work, and make what arrangements he could to attend the funeral of his unfortunate friend.

CHAPTER VIII.

FINIS.

IT was all over. The mortal remains of poor Callander were laid to rest beside those of the wife he loved too well.

The only members of his family who followed him to the grave were a couple of distant cousins. Mrs. Callander was in a strange state of nervous depression. Henrietta in Paris. Dorothy laid up with a severe attack of low fever. Egerton —no one knew where. Of all the pleasant party that used to assemble at The Knoll, Standish was the sole representative.

Those officers who had any acquaintance with Callander, begged to be allowed to testify their respect by attending his funeral.

Then Standish felt he could do no more, and the curtain fell upon the last act of the sad drama.

He was profoundly anxious about Dorothy, and greatly feared her strength would not be equal to the strain upon it.

A few days after he had once more settled to the ordinary routine of his life, he paid a visit to the lawyer at his request, for Colonel Callander, a few days before his unexpected death, had by a codicil revoked his appointment of Egerton as executor, and named Standish in his place, requesting that so long as Dorothy was unmarried she should remain with his children.

Together Mr. Brierly and Standish went carefully through the will, which was simple and reasonable enough. He had little more than a competence to leave his children, but that was judiciously disposed.

The will had been made just before he went to India, and the only changes in it were since the death of Mabel. Then the wish for Dorothy's superintendence of the children was put in, and Egerton's name substituted for that of Standish. This was again altered as described, and a further appointment of Standish, as guardian of the children, added.

"There is no sign of unsoundness of intellect in this," said the lawyer, folding up the document as he spoke. "Yet I must confess there was much in our poor friend's manner and conduct latterly which showed that he had somewhat lost his mental balance. His poor young wife's strange and dreadful end supervening on the impaired condition of his health, would account for much. As we are speaking confidentially, and are equally interested in my late client, may I venture to ask if

48*

it has ever occurred to you that his death was voluntary ? "

" Yes, it has occurred to me ; but, on reflection, I have rejected the idea. The only letter I had from him for some time was just before his death, and in it he spoke of ulterior objects, for which he wished to live. He seemed to have fully intended returning to breakfast that morning. No! I do not think we are at all justified in supposing him guilty of suicide."

" I am glad to hear you say so," returned the lawyer ; " but he had certainly been for some time in a remarkable state of despondency."

" He was, indeed." There was silence for some moments.

Then Brierly resumed : " It has been an extraordinary affair altogether. I don't suppose we'll ever find the murderer ? "

" No; I don't suppose we shall. There never was much chance of it."

" I am very glad Colonel Callander put your name in as executor and guardian. Mr. Egerton was too much a man of fashion and of pleasure for the office, though a very sincere friend—quite devoted."

" Yes, remarkably so !"

After a little further conversation, Standish left him, and walked towards his own lodgings in somewhat deep thought.

He was uneasy about Dorothy, who had not left her room since the day he had broken the news of Callander's disappearance to her. She was very weak, Mrs. McHugh reported, and apparently quite content to lie still, without a desire for anything.

Certainly the doctor assured him there was no need for alarm. It was a case of nervous prostration. As soon as the weather was a little warmer, they must get her away. If fresh scenes, new interests, could be presented, this would, no doubt, effectually restore tone and vitality.

"I wonder if she has any girlish fancy for that young Fortescue? He is a nice young fellow, and in the midst of her grief about Callander, she thought of the pleasure his company had given her. But he is a mere boy; by no means a fit mate for a girl whose mind is as mature as Dorothy's, and quite incapable of appreciating her. What an age it is since I have seen her, and Nurse says she will not be downstairs again for three or four days." Then his thoughts wandered to Dillon. His silence and non-appearance puzzled Standish. He certainly was not likely to renounce the claim he had made for hush-money. He must know well that Colonel Callander's family would shield the reputation of the dead as carefully as they would have guarded the safety of the living. He was up to some mischief. " I should like to see him," mused Standish ; " but I shall not seek him. He will be sure to present himself. He has been well paid so far, but I should like to be sure of his silence. The awful truth must never come out. It is humiliating to think that we are at the mercy of such a scamp as Dillon. But he must be silenced."

Standish here hailed a hansom and drove to his own abode. As sometimes happens, he found his thoughts had been prophetic. The servant of the house, hearing his latch key in the lock, came out of the front parlour. "If you please, sir," presenting a card, " the gentleman said he would call again."

"If he does, show him up," returned Standish, reading the inscription —" Luke C. Dillon." " I shall be at home most of the afternoon."

" The decisive moment has come a little sooner than I expected," said Standish, as he sat down to his writing-table. " How shall I deal with the fellow? he is really master of the situation. I don't want to hold any communication with Mrs. Callander. In spite of all the mischief she has done, I am rather sorry for her. Her son's confession must have been a deadly blow—a blow that must have shattered her pride and ambition, and made the only affection she was capable of a source of torture."

He began a letter to Henrietta, for he was anxious that she should return to her temporary home and to Dorothy.

His lucubrations were cut short by the

announcement of " Mr. Dillon," and the detective entered, fresh, cool, self-satisfied, and red as ever.

" Good morning!" said Standish, rising.

" Good afternoon!" returned Dillon, and both sat down opposite each other, with civil faces and watchful eyes.

" Thought I'd look you up," began the detective. " You'll have been wondering what has become of me ? "

" Well, no ! You see, there is nothing more to do, as——" Standish paused.

" Just so ! Nothing more to do—and a pretty tidy job I made of it, eh, Mr. Standish ? "

" I readily acknowledge your remarkable ability," returned Standish cautiously.

Dillon laughed a short laugh, as if he did not value the compliment.

" Well, sir, the poor gentleman made away with himself sooner than I expected."

" How do you know he made away with himself ? "

" Why, Mr. Standish, you and I, who know the whole truth, need not beat about the bush when we are face to face, and no witnesses by. I daresay there's doubt enough as to intention to entitle you to deny it was suicide, but what you think is another pair of shoes. Between you and me, it's the best thing the poor fellow could have done! His life was over—any life worth living—so he was right to get shut of it."

" We need not discuss the question," returned Standish haughtily. " We are not likely to agree on abstract questions."

" Like enough !" with careless superiority. " Now the reason I have called is to show you that I have a good deal of what I believe you top-sawyers call delicate consideration, mixed with a due regard for my own interest." He paused.

"Pray continue; I am much interested."

"You'll be more so presently. When last you and I had a talk, Mr. Standish, we differed about one or two trifles. One was the amount due to me for information which would certainly lead to the discovery of the murderer, and also for an undertaking to hold my tongue as to the same. Now on reflection I decided not to trouble you. You were not of the family, you could not be exactly a judge of how far their feelings would urge them; so I just crossed over to Paris and asked the old lady, Mrs. Callander, to grant me the honour of an interview."

"You did!" cried Standish. "This is exactly what I should have wished to have spared her!"

"I daresay, but I suspect the old lady

would rather do business with me. Anyway, she saw me pretty quick. Lord, what a taking she was in—shaking like an aspen! She is just fifteen years older than when I last saw her. She's dying by inches, of fright. She soon let out that her son had confessed his crime, and that she was ready to pay me any amount if she could only ensure my silence. But I am a man of principle, Mr. Standish, always was; so I kept down the figure, and told her that two thou. was heavy enough to sink the whole business deep down out of sight for ever. She was quite amenable to reason, not to say in a hurry to draw me a cheque, and wished to add a trifle for travelling expenses. However, I directed her how the matter was to be done; not all in a lump to create suspicion. That's neither here nor there—any way, I have bagged the

cash. Fortunately I got the matter settled
before the news of the Colonel's death
reached her." Dillon paused, but Standish
did not speak. Had he opened his lips, he
felt sure his words would not have been
complimentary. After waiting with ex-
pectant eyes, Dillon resumed once more :

"I thought it right to tell you this, and
as I am just going to start for Australia
on a curious lay—to let you know that
all's square. I needn't tell you, as I am a
man of honour, that you may make your
minds easy, the family secret is safe with
me."

"Unless," replied Standish, yielding to
an irresistible impulse, "some one offers
you three thousand for it."

Dillon smiled, not an amiable smile.
"No, Mr. Standish, my character for
secresy and reliability is worth more than
that!" He rose, and so did Standish.

"Now, I've finished with you, and so I'll bid you good-bye; but I'll not be so uncivil as to put you to the necessity of refusing my hand; though it's a curious contradiction that you disdain the man whose work is so necessary to you in your straits."

"It would be less a problem to you, Mr. Dillon, if you cared to remember that there are more methods than one of doing the work; a grain or two more of disinterestedness alters the aspect of things wonderfully."

"Faith, may be so. Good morning, sir, and if ever any enemy wants *you*, for any little delinquency, pray God he may not put me on your track!" With a defiant nod, Dillon left the room, and by an instinctive action, Standish threw open the window as if to breathe purer air.

*   *   *   *   *

"The day drags on, though storms keep out the sun," and spring was now far enough advanced to make Standish think it was time that Henrietta Oakeley took Dorothy to Switzerland or North Italy. She had been full of the scheme at first, but for the last week or two seemed disposed to postpone their departure, till Standish determined to go and settle the date at which they should start for Brussels, a town Dorothy wished to visit.

It was a fine, bright Saturday, in mid April, when Standish drove up to the well-known house in Prince's Place.

"Miss Oakeley was not at home," said the mournful Collins, "but Miss Wynn is in the drawing-room."

The room looked delightfully home-like; the bright sunshine tempered by outside blinds, the atmosphere redolent of violets. Dorothy was at the piano when Standish came in, and rose with a quiet smile to shake hands with him. She looked less delicately pale than formerly; there was a pale, shell-like, pinky tinge in her cheeks, but, her great dark-grey eyes were more pathetic than ever.

"I am glad to see you at the piano once more, Dorothy," said Standish. "You are a good girl to try and get over your morbid feelings."

"Yes, I must conquer my dread of hearing music," she said, with a slight sigh, "though I don't like to think it is morbid. But if I do not resist, it will take too strong a hold on me. It will not do to be melancholy with those poor dear children."

"No, certainly not. You are looking better, my dear ward," still holding her hand.

"I am gaining strength," she returned,

gently withdrawing it. "This is the occupation that cheers and soothes me most. I must have the soul of a seamstress," and opening a work-basket, she drew out a little white embroidered frock, half made. "This is for Dolly. I am taking lessons from dear old Nurse, who is a past mistress of needlework." She displayed it with a smile, then seated herself on a low basket-chair, and began to ply the needle.

Standish leaned on the end of the sofa, and looked at her with tender regret for the young days which sorrow had so deeply shaded.

"It is time you were away in some sunny new place. Where is Henrietta? I am determined to put matters *en train* to-day, and we can do nothing decided without her."

"I am afraid you will not see Henrietta

to-day, nor to-morrow either; she has just gone down to stay with Lady Kilruddery at Twickenham, till Monday."

"Lady Kilruddery? I did not know she was a friend of Henrietta's!"

"She is going to be more than a friend," said Dorothy, with a gleam of her former fun in her eyes.

"She told me a wonderful tale this morning. She has accepted Major St. John.

"Is it possible?" cried Standish.

"Yes; that was what I said, and you know Henrietta's frank, out-spoken way. 'I really think it is the best thing I can do,' she said. 'He is nice looki ng, and quite fond of me. Then, his eldest brother, the invalid, you know, died about six weeks ago, so Major St. John will be Lord Kilruddery; indeed, he said he would not have had the face to ask me but for this. It sounds horrid,' she added, 'but there is really no harm in it.' So she has gone down to stay with her future mother-in-law. She says she is getting sick of living by herself, and as everything has been miserable of late, she wants a fresh interest; then she is told that Irishmen make rather pleasant husbands, and she will take care he does not squander her money."

" This is, indeed, a piece of news! I hope she will be happy; she is a good soul, though a little flighty," said Standish.

" Yes; very good. How kind she has been to me! I like her so much that I am in a way vexed and disappointed that she should treat such an awful serious affair as marriage so lightly and carelessly. Just think of being tied for life to Major St. John!"

" There are worse fellows. He will let

49*

Henrietta do as she likes, and I think he admires her."

"Ah, well!" Dorothy slightly shrugged her shoulders, and put her head on one side with an air of disapprobation.

"I should like to know more of your ideas on this important subject, Dorothy," said Standish, smiling. "You have withdrawn your confidence from me of late."

"Oh, no," carelessly. "Whenever I fall desperately in love, I shall come and tell you, of course."

Standish did not reply, and Dorothy looked up.

"Why, Paul, how ill and worn you look!" she exclaimed in quite a different tone. "*Are* you ill?"

"Physically, I am quite well; mentally, ill at ease," he returned, and, walking to the fireplace, he stood leaning against the side of the mantelpiece.

" I've got promotion at last, Dorothy. I
am to be secretary of legation at C——."

" At C——? And how long are you to
stay there?"

"That I am not sure—three years, at
least."

Dorothy did not speak. She began to
fold up her work with unsteady hands, and
grew very white, even to her lips.

" Three years, Paul? That is a lifetime.
Henrietta married and you away! What
—what is to become of me?"

" We must arrange something for you,
Dorothy," he said in an odd, absent manner. " I shall not go for a month or six
weeks. He paused; Dorothy rose up and
went to the window, as if to escape his
eyes.

" Though you will not confide in me,
Dorothy," he resumed in a low, earnest
tone, "do you care to hear a confession

of— well, I fear I must call it weakness— from me ? "

" Of course I do," she said, while an awful thought flashed across her. " Is he going to say he is in love with Henrietta? *She* believed he was."

" To you I daresay it will seem folly in a man who has left youth behind him," continued Standish, grasping the top of a chair near him with a nervous grip, "but I have fallen, no, rather *grown* into love, deeper and more intense, perhaps, than many a younger fellow could feel, with a girl almost young enough to be my daughter. I don't know that everyone would think her a beauty ; to *me*, no other face or form was ever so—so fascinating. To sit and watch the endless changes of the one, the grace of the other, is happiness to me. She has her faults ; she is a little hasty, a little self-willed ; but so true, so generous, so unselfish, so kind to *me*; whom she has known all her life. I see her sweet, sad eyes brighten when I come near, but dare I hope it is anything beyond the almost filial affection which might be her natural feeling for me, that speaks in them? Shall I ask her to be my wife? Is it not possible that for kindness, gratitude, pity's sake, she might say Yes, when nature might dictate No? Can I trust her to be true to herself as well as to me?"

"Let me confess, too, before I answer," returned Dorothy, clasping and twisting her fingers nervously, while her heart beat so fast it stirred the folds of her black dress. "I, too, have been foolish, for I have let myself fall in love with a man older, wiser, better—oh, a thousand times better—than myself, and I have been very unhappy, because I was ashamed of loving one who could only think of me as a half-formed, incomplete creature, to whom, however good he might be, I could be only an object of charity in the way of affection or regard. To know he loved me——" Breath and utterance failed her.

"And his name?" cried Standish, imperiously seizing her cold, trembling hands.

"Is Paul," whispered Dorothy, as she gave her soft mouth to his, and leant unresistingly against his breast, locked in a tender loving embrace.

It is well that in this brief, troubled life of ours, moments of pure and unalloyed delight are given once or twice in its chequered course. They may be but short, yet they remain a blessed memory, in heart and mind, like a strain of heavenly music.

"Long, long be our hearts with such memories filled,
    Like a vase in which roses have once been distilled,
    You may break—you may ruin the vase if you will,
    But the scent of the roses must hang round it still."

After a delightful interval spent in a rather disconnected and interjectional review of past experiences, doubts, fears and mistakes, the lovers came partly down to earth. The influence of their old free happy companionship enabled them to speak with complete frankness.

" To think of being always with you, never to be alone and adrift any more ! It is wonderful ! " murmured Dorothy.

" Wonderful and heavenly, Dorothy ! Then, my darling, you will come with me at once ? In this deep mourning our wedding needs no parade, no preparation, and we know each other so well."

" Yes ; that is best of all. I will do whatever you think best. But, Paul, dear Paul—what about the poor dear children ? I must not part with them."

" Why should you ? We will take them with us. C—— may be very cold, but the climate is dry and healthy. We will take all possible care of them, and they will develope into energetic, vigorous young Scandinavians."

" Ah, had our dear Mabel and Herbert lived! How glad they would have been to see us united. If that cruel, dread-Randal Egerton——"

" Hush, dear Dorothy; do not think of him *to-day*. Put him out of your mind altogether. There *is* a Judge who knows the measure of his guilt, and can mete out punishment more just, more subtle, than any *we* could devise."

THE END.

www.ingramcontent.com/pod-product-compliance
Lightning Source LLC
Chambersburg PA
CBHW031421020726
47499CB00005B/1543